My Wish

In the fourth grade, Miss Henderson, our teacher, asked us to write a wishing poem. I wrote:

MY WISH
I wish I could speak to Mary Rose.
That's my name too.
I am named after her.
She died in a fire.
She saved everybody's life but she died
I wish I could speak to her.
I would tell her that I love her
And that I wish I could be like her.
Not to die in a fire
But to be brave and beautiful like her.

Miss Henderson read it to the class, and Danielle Rogers said I was always showing off about being named after Mary Rose.

Other Apple Paperbacks
by Marilyn Sachs:

Underdog
A Secret Friend
Veronica Ganz
Peter and Veronica
Amy and Laura
Laura's Luck
Amy Moves In

The Truth About Mary Rose

Marilyn Sachs

illustrated by Louis Glanzman

AN
APPLE
PAPERBACK

SCHOLASTIC INC.
New York Toronto London Auckland Sydney

ISBN 0-590-40402-4

12 11 10 9 8 7 6 5 4 3 2 1   7 8 9/8 0 1 2/9

Printed in the U.S.A.   28

First Scholastic printing, May 1987

For my nieces Susie, Carol and Amy

THE TRUTH ABOUT MARY ROSE

1

"Let's play Stanley and Mary Rose," I said to my cousin, Pam.

We were sitting on the floor of her room playing dominoes. My cousin held a domino in her hand, and studied the domino track. There was a three on one end and a double zero on the other. She brought her hand down slowly and placed her domino to the right of the three, but then she changed her mind and put it to the left. She looked at it in a worried way, and then picked it up and moved it to the right.

"There," she said, and took a deep breath. Then she looked at me, and smiled. "How do you play Stanley and Mary Rose?" she asked.

My cousin, Pam, has the nicest face in the world. I love my cousin, Pam, so much. I don't think I ever loved anybody the way I love her. Except for Mary Rose, but that is different. My grandmother is always saying, "Blood is thicker than water," and maybe that is the reason. All I know is that when I lived in

9

Lincoln and thought that Danielle Rogers, and then last spring that Lori Schubert was the best friend I could ever have, I just didn't know anything. There's nobody like my cousin Pam.

Since we moved to New York our family has been staying with my grandmother. That's my mother's mother, and Pam's father's mother. Pam and I have tried to be with each other as much as we can. And since her mother and my grandmother aren't talking to each other, I've been spending lots of time here at her house.

Which is all right with me. Her mother is a pain, but her house is great. She is very rich. She has her own color TV set, her own phone, and even her own set of dominoes—ivory ones. There is a swimming pool outside, and a maid inside to do all the dishes. Like I said, her mother, my Aunt Claudia, is a pain, but as long as I can be with Pam I could put up with a lot worse.

"How do you play Stanley and Mary Rose?" asked my cousin, Pam.

"Pam," I said, "I love you so much I don't know what I would have done if I had never met you. It would be like living in a desert, like going hungry, like being trapped in a tunnel with no light."

"Oh, Mary Rose," she said, and started giggling. She really feels the way I do, but she isn't much of a talker.

"But how do you play Stanley and Mary Rose?" she asked.

"You mean you never play it?"

"I don't know how."

"Well, you can be Stanley, since he's your father, and I'll be his sister Mary Rose, since I'm named after her. OK?"

"OK. And then what do we do?"

"Well, we can play it lots of different ways, but let's start on *that night*."

"Yes?"

"Now—our parents are working in the store, and Veronica is at a party, so the two of us are alone. Let's say it's about 9:30, and let's make believe we're—let's see—we're . . ."

"Watching TV?"

"No, there wasn't any TV in 1941. We could be listening to the radio though, and maybe—maybe we could be playing dominoes."

My cousin switched on her clock-radio. Some loud rock music filled up the room.

"Is this all right?"

"I don't know," I said carefully. Mom says I get into trouble because I'm too bossy. And I don't want Pam ever to think I'm too bossy. "Do *you* think that kind of music is right?"

"I see what you mean," said Pam. She switched on

the FM, and finally came up with some slow, classical music. "How's this?"

"I think that's just great," I said. "Couldn't be better."

She started giggling again. Everything makes her happy. She is so much fun to be with. "Now what?"

"OK, now let's play dominoes, and you make believe you're a little kid of six."

Pam is very tall for her age. Both of us are eleven, but she is about half a head taller than me, and I'm not exactly short either. But she scrunched herself together, and blew out her cheeks, and puffed up her mouth. She honestly looked like a little kid. Maybe having three sisters makes her experienced at what little kids look like.

We played dominoes for a while, and then I said in a nice voice, a little higher than my usual voice, and a lot sweeter, "Well, Stanley, honey, I guess it's time for bed."

"No," pouted Pam, "I don't wanna."

She is really tremendous. I had to stop to laugh.

Finally I said, "Now, Stanley, honey, you know Mama said you should be in bed by 8:30, and it's after 9 now, so why don't you get into your pjs and brush your teeth, and Mary Rose will read you a nice story."

"Awight," Pam lisped. She got up, and kind of stamped around the room. Then she made believe she was undressing. Then she came back, and said in a whiny voice, "I can't find my toothbrush."

So I helped Stanley find his toothbrush, and then Pam got on her bed, and I told her the story of *Sleeping Beauty*.

"And they all lived happily ever after," I said. "Now, Stanley, let's kneel together and say our prayers."

We knelt together, and we said, "Now I lay me down to sleep, I pray the Lord my soul to keep. If I should die before I wake, I pray the Lord my soul to take."

"God bless all my dear ones," I said, "my mother, Peggy Petronski, my stepfather, Ralph Petronski, my father, Frank Ganz, my sister, Veronica Ganz, my half brother, Stanley Petronski. May the Lord bless all the people in the world who are good and kind, and may he comfort all those who despair. May he bring peace to those whose hearts are heavy, and . . ."

"Mary Rose! Mary Rose!" Pam said, and she was being Pam. "Do you really think she said all that?"

I was going to say it was my part, and I could play it any way I liked, but I didn't want her to think I was bossy. And sometimes, I guess I do get carried away.

"All right," I said, "let's go on." So I tuck Stanley in, and he falls asleep. Then I go back into the living room, and I read for a while. Then I stop reading. The music is still on—slow and sad—just right. I sniff the air.

"I smell something," I cry. I rush into the kitchen (over near the TV set). "It's a fire!" I say. "A fire! My God, I've got to save Stanley!"

I run over to the bed, and begin shaking Stanley. He is sleeping very soundly. "Stanley," I cry, "wake up, Stanley!" Finally he wakes up.

"Whassamatter?" he says. He is very sleepy.

"Run, Stanley!" I cry. "Run! Save yourself! Run, my beloved brother! Run! I am going to save the rest of the people in the building. Run! Run! Run!"

Stanley runs.

I go around ringing the bells and telling the people to save themselves. I am just about to go downstairs when I remember there are people on the top floor that I didn't reach. By this time, the fire has spread across the landing, and I can't get upstairs. But I *can* try to put out the fire, and save all those innocent lives. I run back into my apartment. The fire surrounds me. I try to throw water on it, but it is too late. I am trapped. I cannot get out the door. The sound of the fire engines . . . ladders . . . hoses . . . I rush to the window, the flames are all around me. Firemen are carrying people out from the apartments above me. I stand at the window. A reporter sees me, and takes my picture.

"Look!" someone shouts. "That child! She saved our lives. Save her! Save her!"

It is too late. The building begins to cave in. I stand

at the window and put out my arms—in blessing, and in farewell. The photographer takes another picture. The building collapses, and Mary Rose dies—a heroine's death.

My cousin, Pam, is crying. The tears are streaming down her face. "You're so lucky," she says, "to be named after her."

I know I am. But I want her to feel good too, so I say, "We're both lucky. I mean just to have her in the family."

Pam nods, and then I ask her, "Are you named after somebody?"

She makes a face. "My grandmother. My *mother's* mother, not my father's."

"No, I didn't think you were named after her."

We both laughed, and then Pam says, "That was beautiful."

"We can do it again," I tell her. "Or if you like, we can do the funeral."

"Really?"

"Sure, and you know what, Pam? Why don't *you* be Mary Rose. Do you have something beautiful you can wear?"

"I have that pink peignoir set I got last Christmas that I never wear."

"OK, put it on, and would it be all right if I made these flowers into a crown for your hair?"

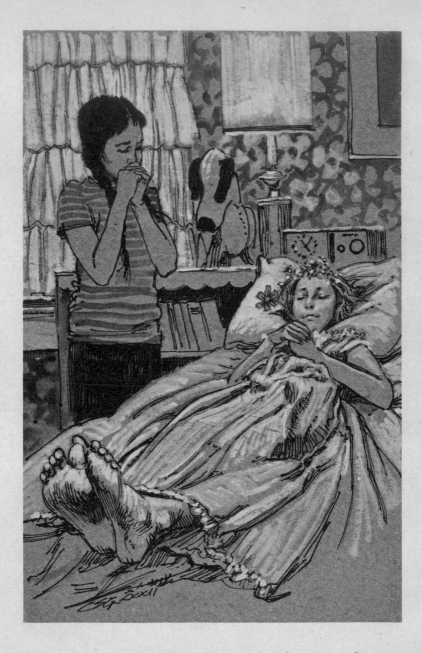

"Sure." Pam carried the peignoir set into her bathroom.

"Your mother won't mind?" I called after her. There were so many things my Aunt Claudia did mind that I had to be very careful. I didn't want my Aunt Claudia to hate me the way she hated my grandmother.

But Pam said there were plenty of flowers in the garden, and her mother wouldn't mind. So I made a crown for her head, and she lay down on her bed, and I put a daisy in her hand.

"Oh, you look great," I said.

Pam opened her eyes. She sat up. She look worried.

"But Mary Rose," she said. "Do you think there really was a funeral—with her laid out, and everything? I mean—was there anything left of her to lay out?"

"You know," I told her, "they can do all sorts of things with bodies. They can make people look like they're not even dead."

"But if there wasn't anything left . . ."

"Did you ever go to a funeral?" I asked her.

"No. Did you?"

"Not exactly, but my friend's uncle died, and she went, and she said he looked better than when he was alive."

Pam lay down again, and I was just about to be Stanley, sobbing by her coffin. But we heard her mother coming up the stairs.

We were playing dominoes again when my Aunt Claudia opened the door. She is a little, skinny woman, but she has a big belly now since she is about eight months pregnant. She says she wants another girl, but everybody knows she only says it because she doesn't think she'll have a boy. My grandmother says it's her fault she can't have a boy. She doesn't believe it when my mom tells her it's the man's genes that determine the sex of the child.

"What are you wearing *that* for?" my Aunt Claudia asked. "And why were the two of you shouting like that before? It sounded like you were yelling 'Fire!'"

My Aunt Claudia always asks the kind of questions that you can't answer. Because if you did, you would sound stupid, and nobody is purposely going to sound stupid. But I am always worried that my Aunt Claudia will begin to hate me the way she does my grandmother, and if anything happened to separate Pam and me, I think I would die. So I try to be very careful when I speak to her.

"Oh, Aunt Claudia," I said, "Pam's peignoir set is really beautiful. She looks just great in it."

Which is true. I never say anything that isn't true. It's just that under ordinary circumstances, I wouldn't be likely to say anything about Pam's peignoir set at all.

Some of the up-tight wrinkles went out of Aunt

Claudia's face. She even nodded at me. "Well, I like a girl to look like a girl," she said.

"Mother," said Pam, "can Mary Rose stay over another night?"

I had already slept over for two nights, and Uncle Stanley was supposed to drive me home tonight after dinner.

"No," said Aunt Claudia, "tomorrow you have to go to the dentist."

"Well, Mary Rose can come and wait. Please, Mother . . ."

I looked away and tried to act like it didn't make any difference to me one way or the other. But I was really the one who put Pam up to asking.

"No," said my aunt. "Mary Rose has been spending just about every weekend here since she arrived in New York. I know her parents want to see her sometimes too." Aunt Claudia laughed.

"No, they don't," I said. "They don't mind not seeing me."

"Well, I'm sure they do," said Aunt Claudia, "and I think we'll just plan on you going back home after dinner."

I looked hard at Pam. She looked at me, and then at her mother. She said, "Mother, why can't I go and stay over at Grandma's with Mary Rose? Grandma always asks me to stay, and Daddy says it's all right with him if it's all right with you."

"Your grandma is recovering from a broken hip, and I'm sure she doesn't need any extra children running around her house. Besides, I can't imagine where she'd put you. Her house is small enough, but with Mary Rose's family staying there, there just wouldn't be any room. Of course, it's very nice of her, and I'm sure she means well . . ."

"I could sleep in a sleeping bag on the floor, and she could have my bed," I said. "Please, Aunt Claudia, I love to sleep in a sleeping bag."

"I wouldn't dream of it," she said.

"But, Aunt Claudia, I sleep in a sleeping bag sometimes even when there's no one in my bed. I love to sleep in a sleeping bag."

"Please, Mother," said Pam.

"We'll see," said Aunt Claudia, "but not tomorrow, because you have to go to the dentist."

"How about next weekend?" Pam asked.

"We'll see."

"Should I call Grandma, and ask her if it's all right?"

"I said we'll see, Pam, and that's *all* for the time being!"

Pam didn't say anything. She is different from me. Because if it was my mother, I'd still be in there going strong.

"And, Mary Rose, make sure you get all your things together, so you'll be able to leave right after dinner.

Now I'm going to lie down and try to get a few minutes rest. It would help if you girls tried to play quietly."

After she left, Pam said, "She won't let me go."

"I figured," I said.

"But you can always come here."

"That's right."

"And, Mary Rose!"

"What?"

"Do you really like my peignoir set?"

"Sure, I do."

"I mean—if somebody gave you one, would you wear it?"

"I would. When I was Mary Rose at the funeral, I would."

"That's what I thought," said my cousin, Pam.

2

In the fourth grade, Miss Henderson, our teacher, asked us to write a wishing poem. I wrote:

MY WISH

I wish I could speak to Mary Rose.
That's my name too.
I am named after her.
She died in a fire.
She saved everybody's life but she died.
I wish I could speak to her.
I would tell her that I love her
And that I wish I could be like her.
Not to die in a fire
But to be brave and beautiful like her.

Miss Henderson read it to the class, and Danielle Rogers said I was always showing off about being named after Mary Rose.

That was when we lived in Lincoln. We probably

would still be living there but one day, last November, my father got a telegram.

I remember it because I was home sick from school that day. I was sitting in the kitchen drinking hot chocolate, and my father was making rice pudding. My father always makes rice pudding when he is worried about somebody being sick.

He was carrying the dish of rice pudding over to the stove when the doorbell rang. You know how it takes only a second or two to put a dish in the oven, but if somebody rings the bell when you are about to do it, you get all mixed up. So the doorbell rang, and my father stood there holding the dish, and not moving. He was thinking: 1) Should he put the dish in the oven, and go and answer the door? 2) Should he put the dish down somewhere else, and go and answer the door? 3) Should he carry the dish with him, and answer the door? or 4) Should he just keep standing there, holding the dish and thinking about what to do?

The doorbell rang again, so I got up and answered it.

A man in a Western Union uniform stood outside. "Telegram for Mr. Luis Ramirez," he said.

"Daddy," I called. "There's a telegram for you."

My father came over, without the rice pudding, and signed for it.

"Go away from the door, Mary Rose," he said. "You'll get a chill."

He looked at the telegram in a worried way. Maybe

24

he thought it was bad news about his son, Philip (my father was married before), or about one of his sisters or brothers. Nobody ever sends him telegrams.

We walked back into the kitchen. The rice pudding was sitting in the middle of the table.

"I wonder what it is," said my father.

"Go ahead and open it, Daddy," I told him. "Then you'll find out."

We both sat down at the table, and my father read the telegram. Then he began to cry.

"Daddy," I said, and I began to cry too. "Who died?"

"Nobody died," he said. Then he laid his head down on the table, and cried so hard his shoulders were shaking.

"Can I read it, Daddy?" I asked. He didn't answer, but he didn't say no. So I picked it up, and read it. The telegram was very long. It told him Congratulations. That he had won first prize in the ARTISTS OF THE PLAINS COMPETITION, and that he would be given a one-man show in the Museum of Modern Art in New York City in February. It also said that the Sheldon Memorial Art Gallery in Lincoln was going to purchase his painting entitled *Interior—7*, and a check for $2,000 would be arriving shortly.

"I don't know why you're crying," I told him. "It's the first time you ever won anything, and you never sold a painting for that kind of money before."

"I know," said my father. He sat up and wiped his hand across his eyes. "I can't believe it."

After awhile, he got up, and put the rice pudding in the oven, and started to do the dishes. I hurried upstairs to the phone in my parents' room because I wanted to call my mother, and tell her. I figured he'd be thinking about how to tell her, and in the meantime I could be telling her.

I dialed the number. Helen answered. "Dr. Ganz's office."

"Hi, Helen. It's me, Mary Rose."

"Oh hi, Mary Rose. How are you?"

"Pretty good. Is my mother busy? Can I talk to her?"

"I think she's looking at some X-rays, so maybe she can talk. Just a second," Helen said, and I heard her call, "Doctor! Oh, Doctor Ganz! It's your daughter."

My mother is a dentist. She keeps her maiden name, which is Ganz, at work.

"Hi, Mary Rose," she said. "How are you feeling?"

"Terrible," I said.

"Is anything hurting?" my mother asked. "You were asleep when I left this morning."

"Everything is hurting," I told her. "My throat, my head . . . and my ears feel like they've got knives in them."

"Did Daddy take your temperature yet?"

"No. He's been making rice pudding."

"Rice pudding?" My mother knew that meant he thought I was really sick. "Maybe I'll try to run home during lunch, and see how you are."

"And bring me some Seven-Up."

"OK, honey. Now get back into bed, and I'll see you soon."

"All right, and . . . oh, Mom . . ."

"Yes?"

"I have a pain in my stomach too."

"Well, I'll be home in a little while."

"And, Mom . . ."

"What, Mary Rose? I really have to be going." My mother's voice sounded impatient.

"I forgot to tell you why I called."

"Why?" Still impatient.

"Because Daddy was crying."

"Crying?" My mother's voice wasn't impatient anymore. "What's wrong? What happened?"

"He got a telegram . . ."

"From whom?"

". . . and that's why he cried."

For a moment she didn't say anything. Then she asked, real slow, "Was it . . . Philip?"

"No, Mom," I told her. "It was because he won an art contest, and they're going to buy his painting for two thousand dollars."

"Mary Rose," my mother said, "are you playing some kind of joke on me?"

"No, Mom, really. I thought it was so great I just wanted you to know."

"Mary Rose," said my mother, "you're a sweetie . . . a honey . . . a darling. Hurry up, and get your father on the phone!"

I ran downstairs. Daddy was sitting at the table, reading the telegram. He wasn't crying anymore.

"Mom's on the phone," I told him. "She wants to talk to you."

"Did you tell her, Mary Rose?" my father said. "Why didn't you let me tell her?"

He picked up the phone, and I ran upstairs to listen. For a while, they were both talking at the same time. My father was reading her the telegram, and she was laughing and saying how finally the art world was coming to its senses, and of course she was pleased, but not surprised, certainly not surprised since she'd been waiting for this for years now, since it was only what he deserved—what he'd always deserved. And he was saying how she shouldn't get too excited. Maybe it was a mistake, and what should they do with the $2,000. And she said—

"Mary Rose, are you listening in on the upstairs phone?"

I held the phone away from me because I figured my breathing was kind of snorty, and maybe she could hear it. Although she often seems to know when I'm listening in—not always, but often.

My father kept on talking and talking. He said maybe he'd have to go to New York for the show in February, and did she think she could go too.

Was he crazy, she asked. Of course she'd go. How could he think for a minute that she wouldn't go.

But how about her patients, he said, and she said, well, it was only November so she wouldn't make any appointments for that week, and if any emergency came up, she'd ask Doctor Bryher to cover for her, and . . .

"Mary Rose! Now I know you're listening. So just hang up! Go ahead now!"

My father read her the telegram again, and she asked him to read it again.

"Oh, Luis," she said, "it's just wonderful. I'm so proud . . . and Mary Rose, if you don't get off that phone, I'll break your neck!"

"Veronica," said my father, "she's not on the phone. I think she's lying down."

"Hmm," said my mother. "Well, I really have to run now. I've got a patient waiting. But I'll be home for lunch. I promised Mary Rose I'd bring her some Coke."

"Seven-Up," I said, before I remembered I wasn't supposed to be there.

"*Mary Rose!*"

But she couldn't stay mad at me on that day. Especially since my temperature went up to 103 by lunchtime, and Doctor Kaplan had to come and give me a shot. I wasn't so happy, but everybody else was, including my brothers, and especially Ray. He's fourteen, the middle one. He was really happy.

Ray's real name is Raoul, but when he started to play on the little league, he changed it to Ray. He's a real great player too. All sorts of people know about him. They say he's going to be a famous ballplayer when he grows up.

Most of the kids Ray knows have fathers who are crazy about sports and are out there playing with their kids or watching them. Most of those kids' fathers go to work every day, and earn money. It always bothered Ray more than Manny or me when kids made jokes about our parents being Doctor and Mister Ramirez. Because, like I said, my mother is Doctor Ganz, not Doctor Ramirez. She's Mrs. Ramirez. But Ray always got upset anyway.

So that's why Ray was especially happy when he heard about Daddy winning the contest. It made him feel good to know that Daddy was earning some money, like those other fathers.

"Wow!" he said. "Two thousand dollars for a painting! Wow! Which one was it?"

"*Interior—7*," Manny told him. Manny, that's Manuel, my sixteen-year-old brother, isn't very interested in sports, or in painting either for that matter. He's serious, like my mother, and we all figure he'll grow up to be a doctor too.

"*Interior—7?*" Ray asked. "Isn't that the one with all the holes?"

"They all have holes," I said. "For the past two years all Daddy's paintings have holes. Where have you been?"

"Yes, I know, but isn't that the one with the great big hole in the center, and a couple of smaller holes up on one side?"

"That's the one."

"Two thousand dollars for a painting that's practically not even there," Ray said proudly. "They must really think he's good."

And of course, it turned out that they did. Daddy's one-man show in February was a smash. One critic thought he was crazy, but all the others said he was great. People started buying his paintings. One of them cost $3,500, and was bought by Bertha Remington, who went to school with Jacqueline Onassis.

In March, my father received an important phone call. He was offered a job, teaching at the Art Students League in New York City, starting in the fall.

"And why?" said my father to my mother that night. They were in their bedroom, and the door was shut. "Why do they offer me this job now? Is it because they like my work suddenly? I doubt it. I have been working like this for twenty years, and they have never showed any interest in me before. Why now?"

"But what did you tell them, Luis?" my mother asked.

"For twenty years," my father went on, "I have been painting my heart out, and nobody noticed. But now, all of a sudden, because a couple of art critics who don't know one end of a paintbrush from another, decide I know how to paint . . . look . . . just look at what's happening! It is disgusting, this art world . . . degrading . . . insulting. I should have been a plumber, or a carpenter—something honest."

"But, Luis, what did you tell them?"

"Do you know what I wanted to tell them?" shouted my father.

"But . . . ?"

"But I didn't," said my father in a lower voice. "I told them, thank you very much. I would think it over, and let them know."

My mother didn't say anything.

Finally, my father said, "You think I should take it then, Veronica?"

"Well, I really don't want to influence you, Luis. This is your decision, and whatever you decide is fine with me."

"But?"

"But, Luis—oh, Luis, you'd make such a wonderful teacher. Just think what you'd have to offer those kids just starting out—help, encouragement, understanding —what you needed and never got. It doesn't matter why and how they offered you the job. The thing is they *did* offer you the job, and just think what you could do with it."

"What about your practice?" asked my father. "We'd have to move to New York."

"Yes, I know," said my mother. "But, Luis, people in New York have teeth too. It wouldn't be so terrible starting over again. I might even take a little time off before I do."

"You're tired," said my father. "No wonder . . . all those years . . . you've worked so hard."

"Of course I have," said my mother, "and so have you. And both of us always will, I hope. You know how I love my work, but I feel like taking a long, long vacation, especially since you'll be making so much money. I could loaf and go sightseeing and shopping and catch up with all my friends and relatives."

"Relatives?" said my father. "You consider spending time with relatives a pleasure? Listening to your mother saying what a fool you were to marry a starving, no-good artist, and a Puerto Rican besides. And on top of that, a divorced man whose alimony you've been paying all these years. You consider that a pleasure?"

My mother laughed. "That's all ancient history. Now that you're famous and making money, she'll probably treat you like a hero."

"It would be worth going to New York just to have that experience," said my father. "So I tell you what I will do. I will take the job at the Art Students League. We will move to New York, and I will bet you a five-dollar bill that your mother's opinion of me will not change."

"It's a bet," said my mother, and she opened the door and landed a sharp one on my backside as I went running off down the hall.

3

Except for the kitchen and bathroom, every room in my grandmother's house had something about Mary Rose hanging up on the walls. The medal that was awarded to her posthumously by the mayor hung over the fake fireplace in the living room. Surrounding it were newspaper and magazine articles that my grandmother had framed. In both the dining room and my grandmother's bedroom, the famous picture of Mary Rose at the window hung on the walls. The photographer had given my grandmother a blown-up picture, which was the one in the dining room in a big, fancy, gold frame. You really couldn't see what she looked like in that picture. Most of it was smoke, and off in the upper right-hand corner, was a tiny figure at a window holding out its arms. Like some of the pictures you see of the Pope blessing the people. But you couldn't see Mary Rose's face.

All of my grandmother's pictures of her were burned

in the fire. Afterwards, she rounded up a couple of baby pictures from her first husband and some snapshots from other relatives. They were framed and hung up in the other rooms, but you couldn't tell from them what Mary Rose really looked like.

My mother said she and Mary Rose looked alike, but Mary Rose was smaller, thinner and more delicate. My mother is tall and thin. She has blue eyes and hair that she said used to be blond. She said I do not look at all like Mary Rose since I am dark like my father, and tall and strong and healthy as a horse.

I always thought I knew what Mary Rose looked like. There is a picture of Joan of Arc in one of my father's art books. She is praying, and there is a light on her face. She is very beautiful. I think Mary Rose must have looked like that. I showed it to my mother once, and she said no, Mary Rose didn't look anything like Joan of Arc. But it's been thirty years since Mary Rose died, and I think my mother must have forgotten.

My grandmother is a widow. Her second husband, Ralph Petronski, died two years ago. He was my mother's and Mary Rose's stepfather, but Uncle Stanley's real father. My grandmother broke her hip in May, so when we moved to New York in June, my mother said we should go and stay at my grandmother's house. She said she would look after my grandmother until she was better, and then our family could find our own place. My father didn't like the idea, but he got to collect that five-dollar bill from my mother. Right away. The first night.

We were sitting around the dining room table. Uncle Stanley was there, and Pam and her three sisters, Jeanette, Olivia and Margaret. But Aunt Claudia wasn't there. She said her legs were swollen, and that the doctor said she had to lie down. But everybody knew it was because she hated my grandmother.

"Well, Lou," my grandmother said, "they certainly are paying you enough to teach art."

My father was looking down at the slice of frozen chocolate cake on his plate. I didn't think it was so terrible, but I guess he was used to his own baking.

"It's not enough," my mother said. She was handing around the cake. "Whatever they're paying him, they're getting more than their money's worth."

"It's like I always said," my grandmother went on. "There's no country like America. It doesn't make a bit of difference who you are or where you came from, if you aren't lazy and just make an effort, you can always get ahead."

My father took a bite of the cake, and smiled at my mother. I guess he was thinking about that five-dollar bill.

"Mama," said Uncle Stanley, "this cake is delicious. I think I'll have another piece."

"Anybody can get a job in this country," said my grandmother. "It has nothing to do with what color a person is, or where he comes from. A man with a family has no excuse . . ."

"Mama," said my mother, "please don't start in again after all these years. Let's just have some cake now and talk about other things."

"But what did I say?" said my grandmother.

"She always says that," Pam whispered to me. Every time she and my mother get together, sooner or later, my mother gets mad, and Grandma says, "What did I say?"

My mother sat down and pulled Jeanette over to her. "When am I going to hear you play the violin?" she asked, smoothing Jeanette's hair. "Your dad says you're very, very talented."

Jeanette is eight, and kind of a prodigy. She plays her violin all the time. Whenever I spend a weekend at Pam's house, Jeanette is always practicing.

"I brought my violin with me," Jeanette said.

"Well, go and get it," said my mother.

"Can we go upstairs?" Pam asked. We went upstairs to the little bedroom where I'm sleeping. It used to be my mother's room. After the fire, her mother and stepfather bought this house, and she lived here until she went away to dentistry school in Lincoln. It still had the same furniture that was there when my mother used it—a bed with a pink flowered bedspread, a chest of drawers, a desk and chair, and a mirror hanging over the chest. Pam and I looked in the mirror together.

"We don't look alike," she said. "You're prettier."

"Oh, I don't think so," I said, although I really am prettier. "And I do think we have the same kind of mouth."

"I'm supposed to look like my mother, except I'm tall like my father."

"And I'm supposed to look like my father, except I'm tall like my mother."

We both laughed, and that's when we started liking each other. Downstairs, Jeanette was playing her violin. Pam closed the door.

"My mother is so happy your family is here," I told her. "She always used to talk about your father and how cute he was. Whenever one of my brothers does something she likes, she always says, 'That's just like your Uncle Stanley.' I guess I always thought of him as kind of little. I had no idea he was such a tall man."

"He's six-foot-four," said Pam. "I think he and your mother look alike even though they're only half sister and brother."

"Hey, does that make us quarter cousins?" I asked, and Pam cracked up over it. She thinks I'm very funny.

After Jeanette stopped playing the violin, we went downstairs again.

My grandmother was saying, "Well, I don't know

why you have to look for another place. You could live here rent free."

"Mama," said my mother, "money is no problem. Luis is making plenty of money, and I'll be starting a practice . . ."

"Yes, Lou is making plenty of money *now*, but we don't know how long that will last. And I'm sure if you don't have to work, you won't."

"I love my work," said my mother. "I work because I want to, not because I have to."

". . . so you could live here rent free, and I could fix up an efficiency apartment for myself in the garage, the way the De Lucas did—down the street—in the pink house."

"Mama," said Uncle Stanley, "would you like me to come and do a little weeding in your garden this weekend?"

". . . plenty of room. You couldn't ask for a nicer place. I could have the upstairs bedrooms painted, and maybe put up new venetian blinds in the living room. And you wouldn't have to worry about the kids. This is a good neighborhood."

"Oh!" said my mother. "And what do you mean by that?"

"I could come the following weekend too," said my Uncle Stanley.

". . . very safe. A nice class of people. But they're all broad-minded. You wouldn't have any trouble with them, Lou, I can promise you that. And, of course, the kids—well, the boys are as blond as you and Stanley used to be, and Mary Rose really isn't dark the way Puerto Ricans are."

"*Mama! Stop it!*"

"What did I say?" said my grandmother.

My grandmother was always saying things that made my mom mad. My mom would explain to Ray, Manny and me that we shouldn't get excited at some of the things Grandma said, and we should always try to see things in perspective. She said Grandma's generation had many prejudices that our generation was free of, and that the best thing was to try not to argue with her.

But my mom argued. She and my grandmother argued over lots of things. They even argued over Mary Rose.

"Not for a minute," my grandmother was saying. They were in the little room behind the kitchen where my grandmother was sleeping since she broke her hip. It was still too hard for her to get up the stairs to the bedroom. "Not for a minute is she ever out of my mind."

"Poor Mary Rose," said my mother. "I wonder what she would have been like as an adult."

My grandmother made an impatient sound. "She was marked from the start. I knew from the beginning she was too good to live."

"Oh, Mama," said my mother, "how can you say that?"

"Now, Veronica, you weren't her mother so you don't know. But I tell you, when I first saw her after she was born, and I looked at that beautiful, little face, I knew."

"Mama, how about a cup of tea?"

"I really can't complain about you and Stanley. And I don't ever want you to feel that I'm putting you down. I'm proud of the two of you. There aren't too many girls who go on to be dentists . . . and who put up with everything without complaining."

"Now, Mama, don't start . . ."

"And my Stanley is no slouch either. He makes a good living, thank God, and he's a good father, and a good husband—too good a husband if you ask me. But like I was saying, you were both very good children. We didn't have any money, and you didn't have what kids have today, but I did what I could . . ."

"Mama, you were a very good, devoted mother, and Ralph was like our own father. There's nothing you have to regret."

". . . busy in the store all the time. If I had only been home that night, who knows . . ."

"Mama, there's no point in ever thinking that way."

"I know, I know," sobbed my grandmother. She was crying now, and so was my mother, and so was I. "But she was such an angel, such a perfect child."

44

"Poor Mary Rose," sobbed my mother.

"I never had to raise my voice to her. Not once in my life. Such a good, happy, sweet child. Always helpful and considerate."

"Mama," said my mother, "she was wonderful, and we all loved her very much, but you really can't say she was perfect or that you never had to raise your voice . . ."

"I never raised my voice," insisted my grandmother. "Never!"

"Now, Mama," said my mother, "you certainly did, but there's nothing wrong with that. Don't make her into something she wasn't. She was a real child with real virtues and real faults, and let's remember her the way she was."

"She had no faults," said my grandmother. "Look at the way she died—saving other people's lives—a child, not even twelve."

"Yes," said my mother, "she had some fine things in her, but I still think we should remember her as she really was."

"I do," said my grandmother. "And she was perfect."

"She was not perfect," said my mother, "and if anything, you yelled at her more than you yelled at Stanley and me."

"I never did," said my grandmother. "Never!"

"Poor little thing," my mother said. "She was so

45

delicate and dreamy and kind of sloppy. She wasn't like Stanley and me. She didn't play outside like other kids. Don't you remember? She used to stay in our bedroom and daydream all the time. She collected all sorts of junk—magazine clippings, newspapers, lipstick samples—and she made up her own world. She kept all that stuff in boxes, and you'd yell because the room was such a mess."

"I never yelled at her," shouted my grandmother. "And she had no faults. You're just jealous, that's what it is. After all these years, you're still jealous."

"That's not true, Mama. She had plenty of faults, because she was a real person like the rest of us. She used to eavesdrop. Don't you remember? It made you furious when you caught her. Just like it makes me furious," my mother said, opening the door and dragging me into the room, "when my Mary Rose does the same thing."

"She never eavesdropped," said my grandmother.

But my mother was too busy telling me off to hear. "All you have to do, Mary Rose," said my mother, "is just knock at the door and say you want to come in and join us. I won't have you listening outside! It's sneaky and dishonest."

She shook my arm, not really hard, but I burst out crying, and said, "You never tell me anything important."

"Now why are you going after *her*?" said my grandmother. "She's only eleven. What's the matter with you, Veronica? Come here, Mary Rose. Come here, darling."

I knelt down next to her chair and laid my head on her chest. She's got such a big, comfortable, warm chest—not hard and bony like my mother's. She knelt over me, and kissed my head and stroked my back, and said what a wonderful girl I was.

After awhile she said to my mother, "I'm so happy you named her Mary Rose. It was worth everything to me. You'd think Stanley with his four girls could have named one of them Mary Rose, but that wife of his—that woman would die rather than give me a bit of pleasure. But at least you did the right thing. You didn't let anything or anybody stop you. It sort of made up for all the years I suffered over you—such a smart, pretty girl you were—and a doctor too. You could have married anybody . . ."

"*Mama!*"

"What did I say?" said my grandmother.

4

My grandmother had certain TV programs that she never missed. Like "The Newlyweds" or "The Dating Game." If my mother was around, she would go out of the room while my grandmother was watching, or if she was in the room, straightening up, maybe, she wouldn't exactly say anything, but you would get the message anyway that she thought those TV programs were pretty stupid.

It was fun when my mother was out. My grandmother would watch all her programs, and she and I could laugh and get excited without feeling there was somebody around who thought we were stupid for enjoying ourselves so much.

My grandmother liked "The Dating Game" especially. She and I always tried to guess who was going to date who. Sometimes she really disagreed with how it all worked out.

"That girl ought to have her head examined," she

might say, or, "I would never go out with a man like *that*."

She noticed the kind of clothes they wore, their hair styles and make-up. She thought most of the girls wore their skirts too short, and the men wore their hair too long. I never thought old ladies would still be interested in dates and dating the way she was.

She told me how she met Ralph, her second husband. She and her first husband (my grandfather, Frank Ganz, who lives in Arizona) were divorced, and she had my mother and Mary Rose to look after. They were both little kids, and one day, she took them with her into the cleaning store. There was a new man working there.

"Was he handsome?" I asked. "What did he look like?"

"Very handsome," she said. "I always went for good-looking men." She giggled, and her old face had laughing wrinkles around her mouth. "Do you remember that fellow on yesterday's show—with the vest and the striped pants? Something like that."

"So? . . . Go on, Grandma. What happened?"

"Well, I put down the coat I wanted to have cleaned, and instead of looking at the coat, he looked at me. And really, Mary Rose, I was worth looking at, I must say. Everybody always said what bright blue eyes I had, but my complexion was very good too. And believe it or not, I never put a thing on my face.

And then, I had this white blouse with a little, lace collar. I was always very particular . . ."

"And then what happened, Grandma?"

"Well, he said, didn't he know me from someplace? He was very shy, Mary Rose, and he stuttered a little sometimes, but anyway, he said didn't he know me, and I said no, and then he saw the children, and asked was I baby-sitting for someone, and I said no, they were mine, and then he got embarrassed, and he took the coat, and gave me a slip, and said to come back on Tuesday."

"But didn't you tell him you were divorced?"

"No I didn't—not then. But I thought about him, because I could see he was a decent, steady kind of a man, and he used to wear this blue and red sweater that his mother knit him. And was she ever a witch, Mary Rose! You have no idea what I had to put up with . . ."

"But, Grandma, what *happened?*"

"Well . . . one day, I guess after I'd gone in, maybe four or five times, and he knew my name. He'd always say, 'How are you, Mrs. Ganz?' And I'd say, 'Just fine, Mr. Petronski.' Well, one day he said did my husband work for the police department because there was a man named Ganz who was a sergeant in the fourteenth precinct, and he wondered . . . So I said no, my husband was in Arizona, only he was my ex-husband, and we were divorced. 'Divorced!' he said. 'Divorced!' Listen to this, Mary Rose. 'I didn't know you were divorced,' he said, 'and I'm so happy to hear it.'"

"And then what happened?"

"Well, what do you think happened? We got married." My grandmother shook her head. "Such a wonderful man he was, may he rest in peace . . . thirty-six years we were married . . . and Mary Rose, I wish you could have seen the dress I wore when I was married. Not to Ralph . . . the first time . . . to Frank . . . all lace and beads. I kept it for years and years. But it went in the fire—everything that was worth anything went in the fire."

I asked her if she ever went back to the old neighborhood, and she said no. Last time, she said, it was twenty years ago, and even then everything had changed for the worse. There was a low-income housing project there now, and she didn't want me to think she was saying anything against my father, but with the class of people who lived there now—it just wasn't safe even to ride around in a car.

We talked about Mary Rose. Sometimes for hours. Especially when my mother was out. I told my grandmother about that picture of Joan of Arc in my father's art book. They were still packed up, but my grandmother said from the way I described it she thought it sounded a lot like the way Mary Rose looked.

There were lots of things she told me about Mary Rose that I guess I knew—that she was kind and gentle and beautiful but not proud. Other things I didn't know. Like she said she had planned on naming her Frances, after Frank's mother, but when she saw how beautiful the baby was, somehow the name Frances did not seem right. And the name Mary Rose just came to her when she was lying there in the hospital.

And wasn't it a funny coincidence that just a few months later, the Queen of England gave birth to a little princess, and what did they call her? Margaret Rose! And if that wasn't a very strange coincidence, said my grandmother, then she didn't know what was.

"But, Grandma, the princess' name was Margaret Rose, not Mary Rose."

"Yes, but it's just too close for comfort," said my grandmother. "I always knew she was marked for something special."

There was another thing my grandmother told me that I didn't know. She said that Stanley came out of the burning building, he was clutching something that he wouldn't let go of until somebody actually had to open up his fingers to get it away from him.

"What was it?"

"A box."

"Of what?"

"Of her things. Mary Rose's collections. You know —she saved things. One of her boxes—of things—like a hobby. I guess he just grabbed at anything, and it just happened to be one of her boxes. When I think of all the things he might have taken—the pictures, especially the pictures, or maybe some of the jewelry. Not that there was anything that was really worth anything—an old gold watch of mine, a cameo pin that belonged to my mother. But naturally, he was only six, so what did he know . . ."

"But, Grandma, what happened to the box?"

"I saved it."

That was when I could hear my heart beating up in my throat. I didn't want to ask her. I was afraid to ask her. Just in case she didn't have it anymore. I wanted to hold on to that thought I was thinking for as long as I could. I wanted to go on thinking that maybe, maybe . . . oh please . . . maybe there was something that Mary Rose had touched, had looked at, something that had belonged to Mary Rose, and would now belong to me.

Finally I asked her, "Where is it now?"

"Upstairs in the attic."

"Oh, Grandma, please, can I see it? Please! I didn't know there was anything left, Grandma, and I'll be so careful."

"But, darling, there's nothing really in it. Just some magazine pictures, and maybe some samples. Things she played with. Nothing special."

"Please, Grandma. I'll be careful."

"Why sure, sweetheart, as soon as I can get upstairs, I'll find it for you."

"But, Grandma, it may be weeks before you get up the stairs. Can't you just tell me where the box is? I'll be careful. I promise not to upset anything. I wouldn't hurt anything that belonged to *her*."

"Don't get so excited, darling. I just don't exactly remember where it is. It might even be in the basement. After Ralph died, there were so many papers and things to go through, I just dumped everything upstairs until I could stand going through them. And then, when the Jacksons sold their house, they asked if they could store some of their things in the basement until they got settled, and you see, they've never come and picked all that stuff up. And now, with all your family's things, I really don't remember . . . But honestly, Mary Rose, there's nothing important in it. I don't know why I've saved it all these years. There's nothing in it."

"Grandma," I said, "could I look for it? Please! I'll be very careful. Just tell me what the box looked like."

"It's a shoe box," my grandmother said, "and now that I think of it, maybe it's up in the storage closet, behind those boxes of curtains. You'd have to ask your father to move them for you because they're too heavy, and they're up too high."

I said OK, I would, and then my grandmother started talking to me about my father. We talked about him a lot. Next to Mary Rose, I guess we talked about

55

him more than anybody else. My grandmother loved to talk about my father.

"I don't get to see him very much," she said. "I don't know why, but he's always out."

"He's looking for a studio, and then he's got to get set up at school, and he's got Philip and our other relatives to see."

"I suppose he's always out a lot. Right, Mary Rose? They say artists are always going to parties . . . and places . . . things like that. Is that right?"

"No, Grandma. At home, in Lincoln, Mom always said he was a stick-in-the-mud. He never wanted to go out at night. Just liked to stay home and watch TV and go to bed early."

"Well, most artists I hear about, aren't famous for being family men. Artists are supposed to be very temperamental, and they have mean tempers. Is your father like that, Mary Rose?"

"No, Grandma. Daddy never loses his temper, but Mom does lots of times."

"She never did when she was a girl," said my grandmother. "But then I guess she had no reason to. I suppose she has lots of housework to do when she gets home. She must really be exhausted by the end of the day. Right, Mary Rose?"

"No, Grandma. Everybody pitches in to do the housework and the shopping on Saturday. And Mom never does the cooking. Nobody can stand it when she does the cooking. Sometimes I cook—I'm not too bad, but most of the time my dad cooks and bakes because he's the best. If Mom makes dinner, it generally comes out of cans or it's those frozen TV dinners. You know —she's been cooking since we got here, so you see what I mean."

"There's not a thing the matter with your mother's cooking, Mary Rose. I'm sure she doesn't like it one bit having your father do the cooking. I for one just hate to see a man in the kitchen."

"Why, Grandma?"

"Because it's not natural."

"Why isn't it natural? I mean if he's a better cook than my mother, isn't it better for him to do the cooking?"

"No," said my grandmother. "It's better for him to be out making money, and for your mother to be home cooking."

"But she doesn't want to be home cooking, and she's a terrible cook."

"It's better for the children, Mary Rose."

"But none of us want her home cooking, Grandma. I mean, we like it when she's home, but not cooking. As a matter of fact, we're all worried that once Daddy starts teaching he won't be able to do the cooking. I guess if that happens, I'll have to do it, or Manny. But, Grandma, when can I start looking for Mary Rose's box?"

"Whenever you like, darling, but first get your father to move those boxes of curtains. I'm almost positive I put it behind them along with some boxes of pictures and letters."

My dad moved the boxes of curtains for me that night. Mary Rose's shoe box wasn't up there. But my grandmother had been right about the boxes of letters and pictures. It seemed as if she saved everything after the fire. School notebooks that belonged to Uncle Stanley and my mother, reports that they made, pictures of them in the years that followed—lots and lots of pictures. But none of Mary Rose.

My mother spent a whole day with me in the attic. She kept saying how silly it was for Grandma to have saved all those old school reports and letters. Some of the letters were from her to Grandma from Lincoln. But lots of them were letters to her from friends when she was living at home. Some of them were from boy friends. There was a whole stack from somebody named Bill Stover.

My mother kept showing me different pictures of Uncle Stanley or herself or friends of theirs.

"Look, Mary Rose, this is a picture of a girl named Lorraine Jacobs. She was just about the prettiest girl I've ever seen. And nice as can be. She married a boy named Frank Scacalossi. Let me see if I can find a picture of him. Oh, look, here's one of Peter Wedemeyer. He was such a good friend of mine. We had so much fun together. We roller skated all over the city. I told you about him, didn't I, Mary Rose?"

"Maybe. I don't remember."

My mother was really happy with all those old pictures. She stayed up there when I went downstairs to watch TV with Grandma.

"Who's Bill Stover?" I asked my grandmother before "The Newlyweds" started.

"A wonderful boy your mother was going to marry —if she hadn't met your father. Now he's a lawyer, and he lives out on the island, and I understand he's worth a fortune."

"That's all right, Grandma," I told her. "If she married Bill Stover, then you wouldn't have me."

"I guess that's so," said my grandmother. "It's like they say—'Every cloud has a silver lining.'" And she hugged me and kissed me, and we watched the program and laughed out loud, and we didn't have to whisper since my mother was all the way upstairs.

5

Every Thursday night Uncle Stanley telephoned. He called to find out how .everybody was, and to say that he would be by Friday night after work. Not to stay for dinner, but just to say hello and to visit for a little while. Aunt Claudia didn't like him to stay for dinner.

After he finished talking, he would generally put Pam on the phone, and she and I would make our plans for the weekend.

"What did she say?"

"No!"

"But Pam, you just have to come this weekend. Grandma says there's a box that belonged to Mary Rose up in the attic. I've been hunting all week, and if you come, the two of us can look for it together."

"That would be great, but she says no."

"Can you get your father to let you?"

"Look, Mary Rose, he just won't. It's no good. He always ends up saying it's OK with him if it's OK with her. And it's never OK with her. So you better come, as usual."

"But, Pam, I just have to find that box. I've been looking for it all week, and tomorrow I'll finish in the attic, and if it's not there I'll have to look in the basement. If I find it then I'll come, but otherwise, I want to keep on looking."

"But, Mary Rose, you can't be looking for it all the time. If you don't find it tomorrow, take the weekend off, and then start looking again on Monday."

"I can't, Pam. I just can't wait that long. I have to find it."

Pam was quiet.

"Pam?" I said.

"I've been thinking about you coming all week," Pam said. "I have a new baby mouse for my Mouse House. I thought we could make some clothes for him, and some baby furniture. And my mother said she would take us swimming at the country club."

"Pam, you know I love to be with you. There's nobody in the whole world I love as much as you. I wish I could live with you all the time, but I just have to find that box."

"No," said Pam, "you don't love me best in the world. You love somebody who's been dead thirty years better than me. You love Mary Rose better than me." And she hung up.

I thought about what she said, and I thought she

was being silly. Maybe I did love Mary Rose, but Mary Rose was dead. The way you feel about somebody who was dead was different from how you feel about somebody who was alive. You could always love somebody who was dead, and you never had to worry about how that person felt about you. That person wasn't going to get mad at you if you didn't look for her box over the weekend. But a living person was going to get mad if you didn't show up.

I didn't find Mary Rose's box on Friday, but I decided to go back with Uncle Stanley on Friday night.

"I'm glad you changed your mind," he said, while we were driving back. They live just over the George Washington Bridge, in Tenafly. "Pam will be very happy you're coming. She sure was mopey last night. Why didn't you want to come?"

"I wanted to come, Uncle Stanley," I said. "I always want to come. There's nothing I'd rather do than be with Pam. I just wish we could see each other all the time."

Just for a second, Uncle Stanley turned to smile at me. "I'm glad the two of you like each other so much. I guess it must run in the family. Your mother and I were very close when we were children. I used to follow her wherever she went. I thought she was the greatest person in the world."

"And Mary Rose too?"

"What?"

"I mean—I guess you felt that way about Mary Rose too," I said.

"I never let her out of my sight," Uncle Stanley said.

"Mary Rose?"

"No, your mother, I mean. She used to get so angry at me. She'd yell and stamp her foot and shake her fist. But she never hit me, and God help anybody who did!"

"She's still like that," I said. "She yells a lot, but she hardly ever hits. But Uncle Stanley, did Pam tell you why I wasn't going to come this weekend?"

"No, she didn't."

"Well, it was because I was looking for Mary Rose's box. You know, the one you carried out of the building the night of the fire."

"Oh!" Uncle Stanley said. He didn't say anything else.

"Grandma said it was a shoe box full of things Mary Rose collected. She said she thought it was up in the attic or down in the basement, but so far I haven't been able to find it."

Uncle Stanley switched on the radio. For a while we listened to the six o'clock news. After the weather forecast, I said, "Uncle Stanley?"

"Yes?"

"Was it a shoe box? I mean, maybe it was another kind of box, and I'm just looking for the wrong kind of box."

"I don't remember what kind of a box it was."

"Do you remember what was in it?"

"No, I don't."

"Grandma said they had to pry your fingers off it. You just wouldn't let go. She said you didn't cry or say anything or ask any questions, and she said the doctor said you were in a state of shock."

"I guess so," he said. "I don't remember." Then he said he was going to buy some baseball tickets for the New York Mets game the next Wednesday night for Ray and himself, and did I think Manny would like to go along.

"Definitely not," I told him. "He hates baseball even more than my father does, but, Uncle Stanley . . ."

Uncle Stanley kept on talking about baseball, and how interested he always was in it, and how happy he was that now he had a nephew who liked to go to games with him, and that maybe he'd try to take a little time, and work out with Ray. He understood Ray was a great player . . .

I could see he didn't want to talk about Mary Rose. And I could understand. If somebody died, saving your life, I suppose you'd never get over it. I think if it was me, I'd want to keep talking about her. I'd want to tell everybody I met how wonderful she was and how I missed her. But I could understand how somebody else might be suffering so much that he just couldn't talk

about it without falling apart. Especially somebody who wasn't much of a talker anyway, like my Uncle Stanley.

So I didn't ask him the questions I wanted to ask. And I really wanted to ask him those questions. Because he was the only one who was there that night, and the only one who could really tell me what I didn't already know.

Pam was looking out of the window when we drove up the driveway. I know she saw me get out of the car, but she dropped the curtain, and moved away from the window so I shouldn't think she was watching for me.

"I didn't think you were coming," Aunt Claudia said. "Pam's been acting like she doesn't have a friend in the world."

My aunt turned her cheek when Uncle Stanley bent down to kiss her. So he kissed her cheek, but she didn't kiss any part of him. My parents always kiss head on. It always looks funny to me when I see Uncle Stanley kissing Aunt Claudia.

"How are you feeling?" he asked.

"Don't ask!" she said. "My ankles are so swollen, you can hardly see my feet."

"Well, why aren't you lying down?"

"Sure! And who's going to give Margaret and Olivia their baths, and take out the dog, and straighten up . . ."

"Well, that's what Norma is for."

"That girl doesn't do any work unless you stand over her."

I went upstairs. Pam was in her room, but the door was open. Next room, the door was closed, and behind it came the sounds of Jeanette's violin. Usually when Jeanette was playing her violin, Pam had her door closed. So I knew she knew I was here because the door was open.

"Hi, Pam," I said.

"Oh—Mary Rose? I didn't think you were coming," she said, acting cool, like she didn't care.

"I didn't come because of you," I told her. "I came because of the baby mouse."

"Oh, Mary Rose, wait till you see him," Pam said. She reached into the Mouse House, and brought him out, and handed him over to me. He was a wonderful little white fur mouse with a tiny blue ribbon around his neck, and little black eyes and a black pointy nose. He was smaller than the mother and father mouse or the big sister mouse.

Pam had two other doll houses. One was a Japanese doll house with a family of Japanese dolls, and the other was an old Victorian Mansion doll house with an old-fashioned-looking family. The Mouse House was something Pam had made herself, and that I had been helping her decorate. The rooms were made out of different sized boxes that you could always move around. Pam, who was on to macramé, had made macramé bedspreads, curtains and wall hangings for all the rooms. She had used walnut shells and anchovy tins for beds, and lined them with pieces of material. I had painted a mural on the bathroom wall—three mouse mermaids chasing a bunch of catfish. I had also made two window shades for the kitchen windows out of toothpicks and strips of gift-wrapping paper.

"What will you do for a crib for him?" I asked.

"I haven't decided yet. I'm trying to think of something that has sides so he won't fall out."

"How about a matchbox? That's about the right size, and then we could glue toothpicks on the sides for bars."

"That's a good idea."

We had to go down for dinner then. The two youngest girls had eaten earlier, so it was only the five of us—my aunt and uncle, Pam, Jeanette and me.

Aunt Claudia kept asking me questions about my father. Had he found a studio yet? How many more paintings had he sold? Was he happy to be back in New York again? Every time I was over visiting, she generally would talk about my father. I guess she liked to talk about him as much as my grandmother did. Aunt Claudia had been studying painting for the past couple of years. She did a lot of still lifes. Usually the ones she did had a vase of flowers and a couple of apples or oranges or bananas rolling around on a table.

She always kept on saying that I should be very proud of my father, and not listen to what ignorant people had to say. She said there weren't many people who had the courage to give up everything for their art the way my father had, and that the greatest artists who ever lived usually were not understood in their own time, and mostly died paupers, and so did their wives and families.

There weren't any empty, small matchboxes in the house, so Pam and I brought a lemon upstairs. We cut the lemon in half, and each of us had to suck our way through to the peel. We would end up with two empty lemon halves, and one of them could serve as a temporary cradle for the baby mouse until we could make him a permanent one.

Sucking lemons also made us feel better. We both needed to suffer since we had made each other unhappy.

"It was my fault," I said, after I had finished. "And I'm sorry."

Pam was still running her tongue around the inside of her lemon half, and shuddering. I waited for her to finish, and then I said again, "I'm sorry."

"No," Pam said. "It was my fault. It's stupid to be jealous of somebody who's dead, and I'm sorry."

"Well, let's both be sorry, and never fight again as long as we live."

"All right," Pam said, "and, Mary Rose, will you promise me one thing?"

"What?"

"When you find Mary Rose's box, you won't open it until I'm with you."

"But, Pam, I have to open it."

"You have to open it just to make sure it was her box, but you don't have to look at what's inside until we're together."

No! I thought inside myself. No! I don't want to share that box with Pam. I don't want to share that box with anybody. I want to find it, and take it upstairs to my room and lock the door. I want to open it slowly, and look inside. It won't glitter like a treasure, I know that, but it will look like something I've been looking for all my life. I don't know what that is, but I will know it when I look in the box. And the box is for me. Because I'm Mary Rose, the second Mary Rose. And she and I are connected in a way that doesn't belong to anybody else.

Pam said, "Are you going to promise or not?"

She was sitting so close to me, I could smell the lemon on her breath. I could lie to her, I thought. I could tell her I'll wait, and then go ahead and look. She'd never know. But I was never good at lying. Mom said listening was sneaky and dishonest, but the reason I always had to listen was really because I am a very honest person. I like to know the truth. Grownups never tell kids the truth, so the only way you can find it out for yourself is to listen. But I don't lie. Even when Mom catches me and asks was I listening. Maybe I won't answer, but if I do, I'll say yes, I was. Even if I know she'll get mad and yell.

So I didn't say anything.

"All right, Mary Rose," Pam said. "If that's what you want, it's OK with me."

I knew it wasn't OK with her. I couldn't stand that it wasn't OK with her. Maybe I'd never find that box, I told myself, although I knew I would. But maybe it would take weeks before I did, and anything could happen in the meantime.

"OK, Pam," I said, "I promise."

Then we compared the two empty lemon halves, and decided hers was the neatest. Mine still had pieces of white along the inside walls while hers was perfectly smooth. We made a little lemon cradle for the baby mouse, and I made him a yellow bunting with purple peace signs, and Pam made him a macramé rug for his room, and we never mentioned Mary Rose for the rest of the weekend.

6

I lost another day looking for Mary Rose's box because of Manny.

Sunday night, after I got back from Pam's, I went to bed at nine. I thought I would get up early next morning, and get started down in the basement. It must have been around 1 A.M., I woke up and was on my way to the bathroom when I heard my parents talking. They were still using my grandmother's bedroom while she slept downstairs in the little room next to the kitchen.

"He said no," my mother was saying. "So I said, 'How about going swimming with Ray?' 'No!' he said. 'Well, then,' I said, 'maybe you and I could go down to the planetarium tomorrow, and Mary Rose could stay with Grandma for the afternoon.' 'I've been there a few times already,' he said. 'I don't feel like going again.' Honestly, Luis, I've never seen him like this. You know, I told you before we left Lincoln that

Manny would be all right, but that Ray would have a rough time adjusting. Was I ever wrong!"

"You can't figure these things," said my father. "Ray had so many friends in Lincoln. Everybody knew him. Look at that party his baseball club gave him, and all those telephone calls! The day we moved, anytime I looked at him, I thought he was going to start crying."

"That's right," said my mother, "but it didn't take two or three days after we got here, and he was off again—playing ball with the two Reilly boys up the block, and going swimming with that crowd of kids from around the corner, and joining the Y."

"It's good, it's good!" said my father. "I'm happy to know that he can get along wherever he goes. And Mary Rose?"

"Oh, her!" I stayed very quiet, held my breath, and flattened myself even flatter against the wall. My mother laughed. "You really weren't worried about *her*, were you?"

My father laughed too. "I guess not. How can anybody worry about Mary Rose?"

"I do worry about the way she keeps sneaking around listening in to things you say when you don't know she's there. I wish I could break her of that. It's gotten worse since we came here, and I just don't understand what makes her do it."

"Well," said my father, "she has to have *something* wrong with her, doesn't she?"

"I guess so," said my mother. "She is really a darling, isn't she?"

Which is one of the reasons why I listen. Because like I say, you never know the truth unless you listen. My mother will never tell me face to face that she thinks I am just about perfect, except for this one fault. Neither will my father.

It was a real windfall that night. They went on and on, laughing and saying how pretty I was, and smart, and funny, and just about perfect in every way, and wasn't it a good thing I was asleep, and couldn't hear them because I'd get a swelled head. Well, I'd heard them talk this way about me before—lots of times—and I didn't have a swelled head. I'd heard them talking about my brothers too. They really liked us. I guess my mother liked Manny the best, and my father liked me the best, and they both worried about Ray the most—so that we all came out even.

But tonight they were worrying about Manny. After they finished talking about me.

"It's not as if he had a close circle of friends in Lincoln. He's always been a loner. And he couldn't wait to come here and poke around New York City. But he's not happy. He's just not happy, and he's never been like this before."

"You know, Veronica," my father said, "I think he'll be all right once we're on our own. Back home, he had a corner of the basement to do his experiments, and his own room to get off by himself. He's that kind of a boy. Here, he's sharing a room with Ray, he has no place to be alone, and your mother—well, he'll be all right once we're on our own."

"But, Luis, you know we can't go until my mother can manage by herself."

"Of course," said my father, "but according to the doctor she should be managing already. You're too good a nurse, I'm afraid, and the patient doesn't want to recover."

"You've been very patient, Luis, and I really appreciate it. I know she's hard to take, and you've been wonderful."

"Don't mention it," said my father. "When your mother turns on the charm, there's nobody like her. And I think it's very considerate of her to circle all the important news items in the paper for me—especially the ones about Puerto Ricans who commit crimes."

I tiptoed back to my room, and had to wait until they were asleep before I got to the bathroom.

Next morning at breakfast, Manny pushed away his bowl of corn flakes. "I can't stand this stuff," he said.

I don't like it much either, but I've been eating it since we moved. At home, in Lincoln, my father used to have hot oatmeal for us every morning, or corn meal mush.

"How about some eggs?" my mother said. "Or maybe French toast?"

My father and Ray had already left, so it was only Grandma, Mom, Manny and me.

"I'll make them," Manny said, but then he changed his mind, said he wasn't hungry, and went upstairs.

"I don't know," said my mother. "I just don't know what to do about that boy."

"Leave him be," said my grandmother. "It's a stage he's going through. That's the way it is with those smart ones. He's a lot like Stanley at that age . . ."

I followed Manny upstairs. The door was closed, and I pushed it open, and walked into the bedroom. Manny was sitting on the bed, crying. I looked away from him, quick, like I didn't see him, and then I walked over to the window and looked out at the yard below.

After awhile he said, "Damnit, Mary Rose, don't you ever knock at the door?"

"I'm sorry, Manny, but I have to ask you something."

I was still looking out of the window to give him some time. I don't remember when I saw Manny cry before. My mother and my father, yes—even Ray, but not Manny. I hated to see Manny cry because I knew when he cried he really meant it.

"What?" he asked. "What's so important that you couldn't even knock at the door?" He still didn't sound right so I kept looking out of the window, and thinking what should I tell him I had to ask him about. All I could think of was Mary Rose's box. So I asked him about that. I mean, I told him how I'd been looking for three days, and how I hadn't found it, and that the basement was such a mess, I didn't feel like looking there, and what did he think I should do.

It was very quiet behind me, so I took a quick look. I could see it was all right again. He was looking at me, and he wasn't crying, and there were think lines across his nose.

"And you say Grandma doesn't remember where it is?"

"That's right."

"Well, that's strange because she seems to remember just about everything else about Mary Rose—everything she ever said . . . every time her nose ran . . . everything!"

I let that go. I remembered the way he was crying just a little while ago.

"So what should I do?"

"Get Grandma to remember. She's got it stored somewhere up there. It's sort of like Pavlov's dog—a conditioned reflex. Use the correct stimulus, and she'll remember."

"Manny, I don't know what you're talking about. But if you could get her to remember, you'd save me a lot of work."

He got up from the bed. "OK." I could see he was interested. We walked downstairs to the kitchen. My mother and grandmother were drinking coffee, and arguing.

". . . it is so because of her. He works too hard, but all she's interested in is money, money, money."

"Mama, Stanley didn't have to expand the business if he didn't want to. *He* made that one cleaning store grow into twelve. *He* wanted it to grow. It's not only her. You can't blame everything on her."

"It's not natural for a woman just to hang around the house and spend all that money, and never go anywhere."

"Mama, she has four young children, and another one on the way."

"It'll be another girl. Just see if I'm not right."

"Mama, how can you keep saying that!"

"Grandma," Manny said, "would you let me perform an experiment on you?"

"Ooh!" my grandmother was pleased that Manny wanted to perform an experiment on her. "What do I have to do?"

"I just want you to do free association with me. I'll give you a word, and you tell me the first thing you think of. Like if I say 'girl' what do you think of?"

"Boy."

"Very good. All right, here we go. Remember, we're going to go very fast. The first thing you think of. OK?"

"OK."

"Black."

"White."

"Good."

"Bad."

"Pencil."

"Paper."

"Top."

"Bottom."

"Very good, Grandma. Now we're going to do it a little differently. We're going to play location. It's the same idea, except if I say something, you have to say where it is. Like if I tell you 'piano', you'd say what?"

"Living room."

"Right! Here we go now—stove."

"Kitchen."

"Bathtub."

"Bathroom."

"Rocking chair."

"Upstairs bedroom."

"Mary Rose's box."

"What?"

"Mary Rose's box. Quick, Grandma, just say the first thing that comes to your mind."

"Well, I did already, Manny. I told Mary Rose that I thought it was in the attic, maybe in the storage closet behind those curtains, but she said it wasn't there. So I thought maybe in the basement, but you know when the Jacksons . . . very nice people . . .

used to live down the street . . . smart girl they had . . . but she never said hello . . . I think she's a teacher now . . . they put all their things in the basement so I . . ."

Manny started laughing. We went upstairs again. "Sorry, Mary Rose," he said, but I didn't really mind. At least he was laughing.

I laughed too. Both of us stood there outside the room he was sharing with Ray, and it felt good, standing there, laughing together.

"You know what, Mary Rose," Manny said, "let's go pack a lunch, and spend the day in Van Cortlandt Park. We'll hike over there, and then later, I'll take you rowing."

I didn't want to go to Van Cortlandt Park with Manny. I wanted to go downstairs in the basement and look for Mary Rose's box. But Manny was looking so happy now, and so sure that I was going to be happy he asked me, like I usually was whenever he asked me to go anyplace with him. What could I do?

The mosquitoes were really biting that day in Van Cortlandt Park. It was while I was scratching three new ones under my left arm that I started feeling sorry for myself. By the time we had tramped over to the lake, and I didn't think it was much of a lake, I was feeling desperate. I knew that I was going to have to get Manny settled pretty soon or I'd be stuck worrying

about him for the rest of the summer, and maybe never get a chance to look for Mary Rose's box.

It was only because I was desperate that I got us involved with Irene and Iris. Manny was rowing, and I was being desperate, when I saw this girl sitting on the bank of the lake, reading. She was a small girl with glasses. Not pretty, but she looked just about the right age. I guessed she was smart—reading there by herself. It was worth a try. Manny always liked smart people, girls as well as boys, and I couldn't think of anything else at that moment.

"Can I row, Manny?" I asked.

He gave me the oars, and was so busy telling me what I was doing wrong that we were practically on top of her before he noticed. By that time one of my oars slapped the water so hard, she got all splashed. She let out a little yell.

"Oh, I'm sorry," I said.

"Mary Rose, give me those oars," Manny yelled.

But I held on to them, and kept apologizing to the girl.

"It's OK," she said, smiling. She really wasn't good looking at all, but she had a nice smile, and did look smart.

"Give me the oars, Mary Rose."

"My brother's teaching me to row, but I'm really no good at all."

"It's hard in the beginning," the girl said.

"My name is Mary Rose Ramirez," I said, "and this is my brother, Manny—Manuel."

"Oh! Hello—I'm Irene Jonas."

"Hi," said Manny, "Mary Rose, just hand over . . ."

"We just moved here from Lincoln."

"Really!"

"Yes, just a month ago. We're staying with my grandmother over on Maple."

"Oh—I live on Spruce."

"Isn't that interesting. We're practically neighbors then." I really had to hold on to the oars. Manny was still trying to get them away. "What's that book you're reading?"

She said it was called *Siddhartha* by Hermann Hesse, and she was enjoying it very much.

"I guess you read a lot," I said.

"Yes, and I've really had a ball this summer. I just finished the whole ring sequence by Tolkien."

Manny let go of the oars, and began talking about Tolkien. I settled back, and started feeling not so desperate. They were arguing about whether *Return of the Kings* was better than *Two Towers*, but they sounded like they were enjoying the argument. Then Manny asked her what school she went to.

"Hunter College," she said.

"College?" I asked. "You don't look old enough to go to college."

"I'm eighteen."

Manny is sixteen, and won't be seventeen until October. I started feeling desperate again.

"Irene!" somebody yelled. "Irene!" and then this girl came bouncing down the path. She was gorgeous, really gorgeous. She had long, long, gleaming yellow hair, which looked like it had just been combed, big yellow eyes, and a wonderful sort of yellow skin. She looked like a cat. "Let's go home," she yelled. But then she saw us. Not really us, because her eyes went sliding over my head, and stayed on Manny. So when she saw Manny, she just stretched her mouth over her teeth, and said, "Hi!"

Manny is very good-looking. He is tall and blond and blue-eyed.

"This is my sister, Iris," said Irene. "She's sixteen, and goes to Stuyvesant. That's one of the academic high schools in New York City."

"Where all the heavies go," said Iris, giggling. She didn't look like a heavy to me. She didn't look like she ever stopped looking inside a mirror to look inside a book.

"Oh," Manny said, "we've just moved here from Lincoln, and I don't know what school I'll be going to in the fall."

"Well, we'll be glad to help you decide," said Iris, "and our advice will cost you one free row around the lake."

She was already in the boat sitting down before

Irene said we shouldn't take her sister seriously, and if we had other plans not to be afraid to say so.

But Manny said he'd really like to, so Irene came and sat down on one end of the boat, and I sat on the other end, and Manny and Iris sat in the middle.

First Iris rowed, and then Manny rowed, and then Iris and Manny both rowed. She was a good rower. I didn't like her—Iris, I mean. Irene was nice. Why couldn't she be sixteen and Iris eighteen, instead of the other way around. It turned out that Iris was smart too. At least she said so, and Irene agreed. She was some kind of math genius, and was planning to go to M.I.T. when she graduated. But most of the time she giggled, and didn't really give Manny any advice at all about what school he should go to in the fall. She said she never met anybody from Lincoln, and she figured nobody really ever came out of such a place alive. I couldn't stand her.

But Manny didn't seem to mind. We all took the bus back together, and they walked us home. Manny asked them to come in, and they sat, and drank Coke and ate fig bars, and listened to my grandmother talk about how it really wasn't safe for girls to go out alone into parks anymore.

Iris tossed her yellow hair all over her face and narrowed her yellow eyes, and said well she had taken two years of karate, and she could take care of herself, but that Irene refused to take it because she said she was non-violent. Which was silly, according to Iris. Because there was no sense being non-violent if somebody was trying to murder you. You only ended up dead, so where did it get you.

After awhile, the two girls got up to go, and Iris said why didn't Manny come back with them, and have dinner. They were both planning on going to see a Shakespeare play that evening down in Central Park, and he could come along if he liked.

"Central Park at night!" said my grandmother. "It's not safe."

"Now, Mama!" said my mother.

"It's all right, Grandma," I said, "Iris will protect him."

Manny looked over at my mother, and she said, "*Mary Rose!*"

But Iris laughed, and said no sweat, she could take a joke. She followed Manny out the door, but Irene turned, and said to me, "Why don't you come along too, Mary Rose. I think you'd enjoy it."

She was nice, Irene. It was a pity that she was flat-chested, and not pretty, and not even as smart or as strong as Iris. And eighteen besides. It really was a pity. Especially since I couldn't stand Iris. But at least I wasn't going to have to worry about Manny.

So I told her no and thank you and that night I began looking for Mary Rose's box in the basement.

7

I found two shoe boxes in the basement. One was filled with old checks, and the other with embroidery yarn. Both of them belonged to the Jacksons.

There were plenty of other boxes—boxes of papers, books, trophies, games, clothes, golf balls, rags, old shoes, and shoe polishes, hardware, Christmas ornaments, dishes, trays and one paint-by-number set. I looked through them all. From Monday night through Friday with time off for a weekend at Pam's house, and from Monday until Wednesday morning, I spent nearly all my time down in the basement. I didn't even watch TV with my grandmother.

"I don't know what you think you're going to find," my grandmother said. "It's no treasure. Just some old magazine clippings."

My mother said she hoped I found Mary Rose's box. She said Mary Rose actually had about ten or fifteen boxes, filled with different kinds of things she collected.

"One of them had all sorts of ideas for interior decorating," my mother told me. "You know she and I shared a bedroom. It was a little, dark room, and it looked out on the backyard with all the washlines. We had some old furniture, and poor Mary Rose was always trying to turn that room into something out of her box. One Christmas, she saved her money and bought a blue satin bedspread, and got Mama—your grandmother—to buy her matching curtains. She was so excited when she unwrapped them, and she laughed and chattered about how beautiful the room was going to be . . ." My mother shook her head.

"Well, what happened, Mom?"

"We made the bed with the new bedspread, and hung up the new curtains. Mary Rose really straightened up the room that morning . . . She swept and dusted and put fresh doilies on all the furniture to hide the scratches. Then we all had to go out of the room, and close the door, and come back in to see what it looked like when you came in from outside."

"Go on, Mom, what *did* it look like?"

"It looked terrible!" said my mother, "worse than before. The furniture was so old and scratched, and the spread and the curtains were so new and brilliant . . . So then she convinced Grandma to let her paint the furniture a baby-blue color . . ." My mother began laughing. "What a mess!"

"But, Mom, what did it look like?"

"It must have been the wrong kind of paint. It chipped, and after awhile, the spread got creased, and Stanley spilled a cup of Ovaltine on it."

"You never told me that story before, Mom. How come?"

"I must have forgotten. But coming back to New York, and having you dig around for that box brings it all back, just like it was yesterday."

"What was in her other boxes?"

"I can't remember all of them. There was the one on interior decorating . . . one on fashion . . . one on make-up . . . one on etiquette. Let me think . . . there was one on hotels, you know, with bridal suites and beautiful rooms where rich and famous people stayed. I think she had one on countries she wanted to visit. Was there one on perfumes? I think . . . yes . . . there was one on hair styles . . . poor, little thing."

That seemed to be the way my mother thought of Mary Rose, as a poor, little thing. Back in Lincoln, when she used to say "poor, little thing," I thought she meant because Mary Rose died the way she did. But now she meant it in a different way.

I didn't like that story about the bedspread. I didn't like it either when my mother referred to Mary Rose as "poor, little thing."

I guess Mary Rose was the only one in the family

who really had taste and loved beautiful things, and maybe there were some people in that family who just couldn't understand. I mean, I love my mother very much, and I think she's great and all that, but I was pretty sure that Mary Rose must have had plenty to put up with from her and Stanley too. Spilling his Ovaltine over her beautiful, new spread!

My room is not beautiful. I mean, back in Lincoln it wasn't beautiful. And my bedspread is washable because, I admit, I can get it pretty messy. But then I *know* I'm not as wonderful as Mary Rose. But I keep on trying.

She would have made that room beautiful, I know, even though my mother shakes her head, and says, "poor, little thing." If she had lived, she would have turned that dirty, dark, old room into something shining and beautiful—like herself. I know!

Wednesday morning, I was down in the basement sweeping up a pile of those little colored pebbles you put on the bottom of fish tanks. I accidentally dropped the bag they were in as I was moving three tennis rackets to get to a box covered with a plastic tablecloth. I heard my mother beep the car horn three times, which meant she needed help.

The car was filled with bags from the supermarket.

"Give me a hand, Mary Rose," she said. "Where's Manny and Ray?"

"Gone. Ray's off playing ball, and Manny is riding the Staten Island Ferry with guess who?"

"She's a nice girl," my mother said.

I picked up a package and headed for the kitchen.

"What a day!" my mother complained, after we brought all the groceries upstairs. "It's just too hot. Why don't we all go to the beach?"

There were drops of sweat on her upper lip, and her hair looked damp and droopy.

"Do we have to go?"

"No," said my mother. "You don't have to go unless you want to. But I think I'll take Grandma. It's just too hot to hang around here."

"Do you need my help? I mean, if you take Grandma, you'll have the wheel chair, and I guess I ought to help."

"No," my mother said. "This time I think we'll try leaving the wheel chair home. Grandma can manage with a cane, and she can always lean on my shoulder if she has to. I'll park up close to where the benches are. It will be good for Grandma to walk. The doctor says she should be doing more walking."

And Daddy's running out of patience, I thought, but I didn't say anything.

"Are you sure you don't want to come?" said my mother. "We'll buy lunch out, and you can swim the whole afternoon."

"Uh, uh," I said.

95

"You look tired," my mother said. She felt my head with her hand. "I hope you're not lifting any of those big boxes downstairs."

"No, Mom," I said.

Of course, what she didn't know was that I was tired from waking up every night about 1 A.M. My father was out so much of the time, and didn't get home until late. I never planned on waking up at 1, but it seemed to work out that way. I'd wake up at 1, head for the bathroom, hear them talking, and stay to listen.

That's why I was tired. That's why I also knew that my father's patience was running out. He wanted our own place. He wanted it very much. He had started to look, and he told my mother last night that she should hire someone if my grandmother really needed live-in help. My father said he wanted to be settled before school started in September. He was going to look for a place in Manhattan. At the same time, he was also looking for a studio. He still hadn't found a studio, and he wasn't happy about that either.

"Well, all right, Mary Rose, and if Daddy should call, tell him not to take anything until he speaks to me. I have something to tell him."

"Mom, why can't we stay here with Grandma?"

"We are, Mary Rose. For a while. Until she's better."

"But why can't we stay here after she's better?"

"I don't think it would work out. It wouldn't be good for anybody."

"It would be good for Grandma."

"I'm not so sure of that," said my mother, "but I'm positive it wouldn't work out all around."

"It's nice up here in the Bronx," I said. "Ray likes it, and Manny does too. I don't want to live in Manhattan."

"Who said anything about living in Manhattan?" asked my mother. "Mary Rose, where did you hear *that?*"

"It's fun being near Grandma. I like it here."

My mother said thoughtfully, "There's a house for rent about ten blocks away from here. A man who's a ceramist lives there, but he and his family are going to Japan for a year, and we could have the house in a week or two if we want it. I saw it this morning. It's a nice house, with a wonderful studio. Not much of a garden, and the kitchen's small, but a really large, light studio."

"I'll tell Daddy if he calls."

"Well, maybe you could give him the address if he calls. And he could go, have a look. Just say it's up to him—whatever he thinks best. If he likes it, he could give them a deposit because I've seen it, and I'd be satisfied."

"OK."

"And, Mary Rose . . ."

"Yes?"

"Just tell him I said it's entirely up to him. Whatever he decides will be fine with me."

My grandmother didn't want to go to the beach without me. She said she didn't like the idea of leaving an eleven-year-old girl alone in a house. Strange men were always coming round ringing doorbells, and looking for an opportunity to steal all your valuables, and worse. She heard of an incident, just a couple of blocks away, where this old, respectable-looking woman came to a lady's door and said she was collecting money for crippled children, and the lady let her in the house, and she must have sized the place up because a couple of days later some robbers broke in, and stole her TV set, and all the watches and money in the house.

I promised Grandma I would lock all the doors, and only open them for Manny or Ray. When they were gone, I went back down to the basement, swept up the fish pebbles, moved the tennis rackets, and removed the plastic cover from the box it was covering. There were some window screens in the box. Nothing else.

The phone rang. I ran upstairs to answer it. My father said, "Hi, Mary Rose. Is Mom there?"

"Nope. She took Grandma to the beach."

"I'm glad," he said. "It's a real scorcher today. It must be about a hundred degrees down here."

"It's not bad up here in the Bronx," I said.

"Well, all right, Mary Rose, tell Mom I'll be home for dinner tonight. It's just too hot to go anywhere."

"Oh, Dad, Mom said to tell you she saw a great house for rent. It's got a really neat studio, and I can tell she just flipped over it."

"Where is it?"

"About ten blocks from here. She said to give you the address, and she wants you to look at it. She says it's up to you, but, Daddy, I can tell she thinks it's fantastic."

"Ten blocks away!" my father said. "I really wanted it closer to work."

"I love it up here, Daddy," I told him, "and Ray and Manny have lots of friends. It would be great for them. And Mom wouldn't have to worry about us up here."

"Mary Rose," said my father, "you're beginning to sound like your grandmother."

"Oh, Daddy, please!"

"Well, I'll go and look at it, but . . ."

"Mom says it's up to you, but if you like it you can leave a deposit, because she says it's super fantastic."

"She said *that!*"

"No, but I know she thinks so." I gave my father the address, and hung up.

It was so hot! It was hard just holding your head up. My grandmother didn't have air conditioning. She said it wasn't healthy. But she had one of those big floor fans in the living room. I turned it on, and sat up close to it. I could feel the cool blast of air drying off the wet spots on my face, and under my hair. I thought what now? Where do I go. I've looked everywhere in the attic, and everywhere in the basement, and I can't find it. I let the wind blow in my face, and I couldn't think of what to do next.

I closed my eyes, and I said to myself, I will count to three, and when I say three, it's going to come to me where Mary Rose's box is. So I closed my eyes, and counted . . . 1 . . . 2 . . . 3 . . . I opened my eyes but the cold air from the fan was coming at me too fast, and my eyes hurt. I turned off the fan, closed my eyes, and counted again . . . 1 . . . 2 . . . 3 . . .

This time, I kept my eyes closed, and listened. That heavy stillness felt like it was wrapping itself around my head, but I didn't open my eyes. Where is it? Where is Mary Rose's box?

There was a noise in the room, out of the heat and the quiet air. I was so frightened that I opened my eyes, but there wasn't anything. I didn't want to close my eyes again. I didn't know what had made that noise, or maybe I did know or thought I knew, but I was afraid to close my eyes.

I put the fan on again, and the noise of it whirring made me feel better. I walked upstairs to the attic. All of the boxes of photographs and letters and papers had been put into piles by my mother. One of them said, "Check with Stanley." Another one said, "Veronica," and another one said, "Mama—throw these out?" I looked up in the storage closet but there weren't any boxes there. The three large boxes containing the curtains stood in front of the closet waiting for my father to put them back on the shelf.

My grandmother had said, "Behind the curtains," and I'd already looked.

Behind the curtains.

You just couldn't expect old ladies to remember everything.

Behind the curtains.

I opened the first box, and yanked out some heavy wine-colored drapes with a faded pink lining. There were several of them in the box, and nothing else. The second one had those frilly sheer curtains that old ladies hang up in their kitchens. There was a pair of white ones with blue-checked borders, and a pair of yellow ones with daisies, some bathroom curtains, green and shiny and wet smelling, and down at the very bottom—was Mary Rose's box.

Behind the curtains.

The first thing I did, before I opened it, because I knew it was her box, the first thing I did, was to kiss it.

But I didn't open it right away. After I kissed it, I rubbed my hands over it. It felt like any other

shoe box, but older. I'm holding a box that's thirty years old in my hands, I thought. I'm holding Mary Rose's box.

The box had TRED-RITES written in the middle. It was a yellow box, but the color was an old yellow, and there were blue shoes walking around the border of the box top. On the side of the box, it said:

LDS. RD. SNKR.

5

It must have been a box that once had held a pair of shoes worn by Mary Rose. Five must have been her shoe size. She was my age when she died, a little older, because she was nearly twelve and I am just eleven and a half. But she wore a size five. I wear a six and a half. Her foot, I thought, must have been small and slim and beautifully shaped.

There was a lot of string around the box to keep the top on, and the contents from spilling out. I took off the string, and lifted the cover.

It was Mary Rose's box. I knew it was Mary Rose's box before I opened it. And it was her treasure box. There were gold rings, watches, ruby necklaces, diamonds—lots and lots of diamonds, pearl chokers, sapphire bracelets, solid gold charms and rings. I didn't take any of them out of the box then but I put my hands in, and felt how cool and smooth they were. One of the gold rings I slipped on my finger, and I thought, I'm wearing a ring that Mary Rose wore. I moved the ring off my finger, covered up the box, and slipped the string back over it.

I carried the box down the stairs with me to my bedroom. I locked the door, and spread them out one by one on my bed. They didn't all fit, so I put some of them on the floor, and sat in the middle of Mary Rose's treasures. Some of them had faded, on others the paper was stiff, and beginning to crumble. But most of them were still as bright and shiny as when she first cut them out of the magazines thirty years ago.

8

I didn't know what I was going to tell Pam—
I mean about how I opened Mary Rose's box and
didn't wait for her. I never should have promised.
I know that. It's like promising you're not going to
breathe or you're not going to sleep.

That night, when it was bedtime, I put everything
back in the box. But I couldn't sleep. It came one
o'clock, and I listened to my parents' conversation
as usual. Daddy said OK about the house, and Mom
kept saying was he absolutely sure it was all right.
She wouldn't mind at all living in Manhattan, and
she realized that living up here in the Bronx would
mean a long trip for him every day on the subway.
He said no, the studio was fine, and if she liked the
house and the neighborhood, that was fine too. Then
she said well how did he feel about living so close
to her mother. He said that was fine too. And then
my mother said, "What's wrong, Luis?"

It seemed there were a whole lot of things wrong.

First of all, my father was disappointed in what was happening between him and his son, Philip. He had been looking forward to New York because he thought it would give him a chance to spend a lot of time with Philip. But although he still wanted to spend a lot of time with Philip, Philip didn't seem to want to spend much time with him. And when they were together, there didn't seem much to talk about.

Then there was the New York Art World. My father hated it. He hated the people and the talking and the parties and the money, and most of the work other artists were doing. I guess he hated just about everything. He had just sold another three paintings, and tomorrow a reporter was coming to see him from an art magazine to do an article on him, and he hated that too. And then, he wasn't painting. He hadn't painted since we came to New York.

My mother said she thought most of the problems would fall into line once we were settled in our own place. But if not, she wanted my father to remember that we weren't married to New York and could always go back to Lincoln next summer.

They talked for a long time, but the important thing was that we were going to live in that house up here in the Bronx, and be close to my grandmother. Which made me feel pretty good.

But I still couldn't sleep. So after they were asleep, I got up, and opened Mary Rose's box again. I took everything out, one by one, and tried everything on that was meant to be tried on. Mary Rose had cut most of the jewels out so that she could wear them. If it was a ring, she cut out the center part so it would fit around her finger. With the necklaces, she usually pasted on extra strips of paper and attached the ends so she could slip them over her head. Sometimes she used clear tape or stamp hinges. Just about all of them had fallen off or hung there, dry and brittle. But I could slip them over my head and hold them with one hand. Some of the bracelets were like the rings. You could slip your fist through them. The pins, I guess, she just held up to herself, although some of them had dried up pieces of tape on the backs.

There was a diamond tiara that Mary Rose had pasted on a paper band that must have fit on her head. It was crushed flat by the weight of all the other cutouts that rested on top of it. When I opened it out, the paper on the sides looked like it would crumble. I slipped the tiara on my head, very carefully, and I looked at myself in the mirror. The tiara had a huge diamond in the center, and spears of diamonds that grew smaller and pointier toward the tops. All of the tops drooped now, but I squinted my eyes, and made myself blurry in the mirror, and there was Mary Rose, pale and beautiful, wearing her sparkling, pointed tiara, and looking like a queen.

Then it came apart. I thought about taping it back together again. It didn't seem right to put today's tape on Mary Rose's treasures. I put it down, and went back to taking out the other things.

There were a few whole ads from magazines. There was one of a man and a woman kissing. The woman had her arm around the man's neck. The arm had a watch on it, and the advertisement said, "A thousand tender words in one—$35."

There was another one of a sexy, red-haired woman with a tight, low-cut dress, holding out her hand and smiling at a ring with a great big diamond. The advertisement said, "Jewelry of the future—RHINESTONE— clear-cut and dazzling as an iceberg in sunlight—modern, unashamedly enormous—This supercolossal ring *only* $10."

Mary Rose had written something on this ad. It was the only one where she had. She had made an arrow pointing to the woman's head, and above it, she had written "Me." She had written the "Me" with lots of swirls, and there was an exclamation point after it that was also fancy. The whole thing looked like this

It was beautiful. It was the only writing I had that came from Mary Rose herself. I couldn't figure why she wrote "Me" over that red-headed woman because I knew Mary Rose didn't look anything like *that*. Maybe it meant that she wished she had a diamond ring too, or maybe she wished she was a grownup. Probaby there was something about that woman in the picture that Mary Rose knew, and I didn't know, that made her write "Me." Like she might have been somcone who was a famous musician, or maybe a rich lady who gave lots of money for starving children.

There was no point in thinking about it. I was so happy to have her writing. It was the greatest treasure to me in Mary Rose's box. Her own writing!

There was something else in the box that I couldn't figure. There were about thirty of those paper rings that go around cigars. They are really paper bands that keep cigars wrappcd up in clear plastic paper. When you pull off the ring, the paper comes off too. There were thirty of them in Mary Rose's box, all of them the same. They had the name EL CAPITAN stamped in the middle, and they were all red with gold borders and a picture of a gold lion holding a gold banner in the center.

My father never smoked cigars, but I had seen those paper cigar rings before. I knew you could slip them on your fingers. Mary Rose had glued the backs of them, and they were all flattened out and looked mashed.

It seemed strange that she would have kept them in the midst of all those real jewels. I mean they weren't real either, being paper, but they were pictures of real things, and the cigar rings were only cigar rings.

My mother came up the next day, and looked at all the jewels in Mary Rose's box. She began shaking her head. I knew she was going to start again about Mary Rose being a "poor, little thing," and I didn't want to hear that. So I said, "Mom, where did these cigar rings come from?"

"Ralph smoked cigars," my mother said. "Not that often, but on special occasions. I guess he must have given her the rings. I don't really remember."

That evening, Uncle Stanley called. This time he had some other news to tell. Aunt Claudia was in the hospital, and there was a new addition to the family. His name was Ralph Edward, and he weighed 8 pounds 2 ounces.

"About time too," said my grandmother. But then she began to cry, and said she was happy that it was a boy, and she was even happier that his name was Ralph.

She and my mother drove to the hospital, and I couldn't help noticing that my grandmother walked very quickly down the stairs, and didn't really seem to need her cane at all.

Uncle Stanley came back with them.

"I never saw a baby like this one," said my grandmother. "He's the image of Stanley, and has the most beautiful, little face you ever saw. All those people looking in the nursery window, you could just see they couldn't take their eyes off him."

Uncle Stanley laughed. "Oh, Mama, you know that's not so."

"Now, Stanley, it's not because he's mine. You know I'm not like that. I always say what's true, and I tell you I never saw such a gorgeous baby in my entire life."

"And when Margaret was born . . . ?" Uncle Stanley said.

"Well, it was true. She had a head of curls on her, Veronica," said my grandmother, "I wish you could have seen her. And I know newborn babies aren't supposed to smile, but I tell you that Margaret was smiling."

Uncle Stanley laughed some more. He was very happy. My mother got up, and hugged and kissed him, and he didn't seem at all embarrassed.

"I'll get a few things together, Stanley," my mother said, "and we'll go. Come on, Mary Rose."

"Where are we going?"

"Oh, I forgot to tell you. Stanley's baby-sitter can't stay tonight or tomorrow. She'll come back on Saturday, and I thought we'd go along and fill in. There's plenty of food here, and both Manny and Ray are planning to be home tomorrow. Manny can cook— I know he'd enjoy staying with Grandma—right, Manny?"

"Right," Manny said, in a low voice with a tight smile.

"And Ray too," said my mother. "Right, Ray?"

"Oh, sure," said Ray.

"I could stay," I said. "I *like* to take care of Grandma."

"That's all right," said my mother. "I know how much you look forward to seeing Pam, and how much she looks forward to seeing you. The boys can manage, and Daddy will be in and out too."

"I'm so lucky," my grandmother said, reaching out, and taking Manny's hand. He kept smiling, but he wasn't exactly looking at her. She turned and smiled at Ray, and reached out a hand for him too. So he came over after a minute, and took her hand, and stood sideways near her chair.

"I'm a very lucky woman," my grandmother said. "My children are good to me, and my grandchildren can't do enough for me." She started crying. "I'm so lucky . . . if Mary Rose could only have lived . . ."

I put Mary Rose's box in my overnight bag. Sooner or later, Pam was going to have to know, so I might as well get it over with. I just hoped she wouldn't stay mad. I couldn't live if she stayed mad.

Jeanette was not playing her violin when we arrived. All the girls were in the kitchen putting blue frosting on a cake.

"It's for you to take to the hospital tomorrow for Mom," Jeanette said.

"We're going to put blue sugar over it," Olivia said.

"And the baby can have a piece too," said Margaret.

She really was a very pretty little girl, and did have a wonderful head of dark, shiny curls.

My mother picked her up, and hugged her. "And who's going to be a great big sister, and take care of her little baby brother?"

"Me!" said Margaret, looking shy, and laying her cheek down on my mother's shoulder.

"And me too," said Olivia. She's six, and not as pretty as Margaret, but everybody says she's brilliant. She can read any book in the house, and knows all the multiplication tables. She's very jealous of Margaret, even though Margaret doesn't seem at all smart —just pretty. She pulled my mother's arm, and pushed at Margaret's feet.

So Uncle Stanley picked Margaret up, and my mother sat down, and took Olivia into her lap.

I looked over at Jeanette. After all, she's only eight. But she was busy sprinkling blue sugar over the cake, and didn't seem at all jealous.

"Congratulations," I said to Pam.

"For what?"

"For having a baby brother."

"Oh that!"

"Aren't you happy?"

"Sure."

"You don't look happy," I said as we started upstairs.

"Oh, it's all right," she said. She was quiet for a moment, then she said, "So what's so special if it is a boy? They're all acting like they never saw a boy before in their lives." She kicked one of the steps.

She was hurting. I loved my cousin, Pam, so much I could feel the hurt inside me too. "It's not that he's a boy," I told her. "It's just that he's different. I mean, they have four girls, so naturally they wanted a boy. I mean, if they had four boys, they'd want a girl. I mean, it's nothing personal."

She nodded, and her mouth shook a little bit. Then she said, "Mary Rose, I'm so glad you came."

"Me too," I said, "and you know what?"

"What?"

"I brought something."

"What?"

"Mary Rose's box."

"No kidding," she yelled. "You found it? Where?"

"Well, it actually *was* in the storage closet in the attic, just like Grandma said," I told her. "And you know she said it was behind the drapes?"

114

"Yes?"

"Well it was underneath them. You know, depending on how you look at it—underneath is really behind —in a way."

"How wonderful!" Pam said, "and we can open it today, and lock the door, and not let anybody into my room, and we'll be the only ones who know. Right, Mary Rose?"

"Oh—right, Pam!"

I wasn't going to tell her that I already knew what was in the box, and so did my mother, and our grandmother too. She was feeling so good now, I didn't want to remind her about having a brother and feeling so lousy. So I just didn't say anything. What was the hurry? I could tell her another time. When she was feeling better.

Pam locked her door, and then we opened the box. We spread the rings and bracelets and necklaces and watches and the diamond tiara all over Pam's floor. They didn't look right on Pam's floor. They didn't look right either when Pam tried them all on herself. And laughed, and said what corny looking things they were.

I didn't like the way she made faces at herself in the mirror, and I didn't like it when she said that "Me" over the red-headed woman meant that Mary Rose wanted to look like that when she grew up.

I think I would have said something even though

I was trying to be careful, but somebody knocked on the door.

"Stay out!" Pam said.

"It's me, Pam," said Uncle Stanley. "May I come in for a minute?"

"Sure, Daddy, just a second," Pam had slipped one of those cigar bands on each of her fingers, and was wearing two bracelets on her arm and a string of copper-colored pearls.

She got up, opened the door, and Uncle Stanley came into the room. He was still smiling. "Mom wants me to bring her pink slipper socks, but I can't find them. Do you know where she keeps them?"

"They're in the third drawer of her dresser—where she keeps her tights and stockings."

Uncle Stanley kept smiling at Pam. He looked at me, and smiled at me too. Then he turned back to Pam, and smiled some more at her. "What are you two doing?" he asked. "Dressing up?"

Pam put her hands up, and patted the string of copper-colored pearls. Uncle Stanley smiled at the string of pearls. Then he looked at the cigar rings on Pam's fingers, and when you read in books about a smile fading, that is just what happened on Uncle Stanley's face. It started fading in the middle. The center of his mouth came straight before the ends. It was all gone finally, but he still kept looking at those cigar rings.

"Where did you get them?" he said finally.

"Out of Mary Rose's box," said Pam. "Isn't it all right? Grandma told Mary Rose she could look for it, and she did, and she found it. We were just looking at what was inside. Is it all right, Daddy?"

"Oh sure, sure," said Uncle Stanley. "It's fine." He smiled again, but it wasn't like the other smile. "I'll go get Mom's slipper socks now," he said.

"I think it reminds him of her," I told Pam after he left. "I notice he never likes to talk about her."

"Maybe so," Pam said, slipping off the rings and putting them back in the box. She took off the bracelets and the string of copper-colored pearls, and put them back in the box. "Grandma was right. There really is nothing special here—just some faded old cutouts. It gives me the creeps." She handed me Mary Rose's box. "Let's do something interesting," my cousin Pam said. "Let's play with the Mouse House."

9

The house was very quiet when I woke up, with that heavy kind of quiet you hear when people are sleeping. But there was a stirring inside the quiet so that I knew somebody was talking.

Pam was asleep, lying straight and important-looking in the middle of her canopied bed. I opened the door, and tiptoed out to the landing and listened. They were downstairs in the kitchen. Somebody laughed—my mother, and somebody else laughed too—Uncle Stanley.

I came down the stairs, resting on each step until my movement became part of the quiet. They were in the kitchen, and the laughing and the talking began to shape up as I moved down the stairs. First it was only separate words, ". . . car . . . hurry . . . drop . . ." Then groups of words, ". . . she said to me . . . I don't know where . . . check with the nurse . . ." And then sentences, "Don't forget to call

Mrs. James," and, "The first time it was different."

They were talking about Aunt Claudia and the new baby. I stood on the bottom step, and knew it wasn't safe. They couldn't see me from the kitchen, but if one of them was to come out into the hall, I'd be exposed.

Under the staircase was a large clothes closet. The door was slightly opened. Good! I moved toward it, hugging the side of the staircase. When I reached the closet, all I had to do was expand the opening and slip inside. It was a very glamorous closet with a fancy pink phone on a lavender table, and a matching bench with lavender and white striped cushions. It was the first time I ever listened in such comfort. I sat down, and pushed the door open a little more. Both my mother and Uncle Stanley have loud voices, even when they speak softly.

". . . was surprised," Uncle Stanley was saying, "because I really didn't think I'd be able to stand there without getting upset."

"Luis wouldn't," my mother said.

"I didn't want to either, but Claudia wanted to take the course, and then it meant so much to her that I went along too."

"Natural childbirth is the best thing for the baby, and I really do think it's important for the father to be part of the birth too," said my mother.

"It was beautiful," Uncle Stanley said, "and Claudia

was wonderful. It didn't take very long, and she did everything the doctor told her—no fussing at all except when they were wheeling her into the delivery room. She started yelling suddenly. Naturally, I thought it was from the pain, but no, she was yelling, 'My glasses, my glasses! I left my glasses! Hurry, I need my glasses! Hurry!'"

My mother laughed.

"She wanted to see it all," Uncle Stanley said, "and it was worth seeing. I tell you, Veronica, when they held that baby up, even before I knew it was a boy, and he was kind of blue, and moving in a sleepy way—I never felt anything like I felt when I saw *that!*"

It sounded like Uncle Stanley was crying, and for a while, nobody said anything. Then my mother said, "I'm happy for you, Stanley. I'm glad you have a boy. I guess you really wanted him."

"And how!" from Uncle Stanley.

"Like Luis and me, before Mary Rose was born. We wanted a girl so badly, we wouldn't even admit it to each other. We both kept saying how we really wanted another boy, and how girls were such a pain to bring up."

I patted myself on the head, and grinned.

"She's a beautiful girl," Uncle Stanley said, "and so bright. And your boys! Such wonderful boys! Manny is brilliant, and that Ray—I just hope my . . . my son grows up to be like your Ray."

"And Mama's so happy," my mother said.

"Oh, Mama!" Uncle Stanley said, and the two of them laughed like they knew something nobody else did.

"She's really pleased you named the baby Ralph."

"Papa was wonderful," Uncle Stanley said. "How could I name him anything else?"

"He certainly was wonderful," said my mother. "And he was so good to Mary Rose and me. We never felt left out. He was like a real father."

They were quiet again, and then my mother said did he want some more coffee, and he said yes, and she said she would too. There was some clinking and clattering, and I began feeling very sleepy. Then he said, "*You* never felt left out."

"What?"

"I mean *you* never felt my father favored me over you."

"Oh, Stanley, you were so little and so cute. You were the baby. Remember I was eight when you were born, and Mary Rose was six. So it was natural that everybody was going to make a little extra fuss over you. We did too. We didn't mind."

"*You* didn't mind."

"No, and neither did . . ."

"She did, she did!" he said, and he sounded like a little kid. Something fell on the floor, and my mother said watch out, she'd sweep it up. Then there were some sweep-up noises, and him saying how clumsy he always was, especially when he was upset. I started feeling hot and uncomfortable. I had this feeling like I ought to go upstairs now. Like whatever I wanted to hear, maybe I'd heard it already.

"You're excited," my mother said softly. "It's natural. And then you didn't sleep last night at all, and you have a new son to think about. We're all excited."

Uncle Stanley said, "After each girl was born, I knew she was going to be unhappy."

"Who?"

"Mama."

"I don't know why you say that, Stanley. She loves the girls. Of course, she wanted you to have a boy too, but she's always talking about Jeanette and . . ."

"I mean she was unhappy because we didn't name any of them Mary Rose."

"Well, don't worry about that. You know Mama when it comes to Mary Rose."

"She thinks it's because Claudia didn't want to."

"And why should she?"

"But it wasn't Claudia. As a matter of fact, when Olivia was born, she even said, 'Why don't you make your mother happy and name her Mary Rose?' It wasn't Claudia. It was me."

My mother said slowly, "You were so little when it happened. Something like that will always stay with

you. I guess it hurts too much for you to want a constant reminder. I understand, Stanley, and I think Mama would too if you explained it to her."

I was nodding inside the closet. Of course that was it. Of course. The way he never wanted to talk about her. The way he always avoided thinking about her. The way, before, he couldn't stand looking at the cigar rings on Pam's fingers. Now go upstairs, I told myself. Don't listen anymore. This is what it's all about. Go upstairs!

But I didn't.

"Each time," he said, and you could hear that he was beating a spoon on the table, "it was a girl, I'd think about how she was going to be unhappy, and each time I knew I couldn't do anything about it."

"Stanley, I know you'd feel a lot better if you told her."

"No, Veronica, you don't know. You're wrong. Even before—upstairs—Pam and Mary Rose were playing with —those things from her box. I couldn't stand it. I remembered all over again."

My mother laughed, but it wasn't a comfortable laugh. "My Mary Rose has this thing about Mary Rose. She's been searching for that box since she heard about it. She thinks poor Mary Rose was some kind of Joan of Arc figure—a great and wonderful heroine. She's always at me to tell her stories about

Mary Rose, and I try to tell her what she was really like. But Mary Rose has a way of listening only to what she wants to hear. I guess it's not good, but children are going to idealize someone, and they grow up soon enough."

"Pam was wearing those cigar rings from Papa's cigars."

"Poor boy!" my mom said. "I guess you'll never forget that night."

"I'll never forget Mary Rose," Uncle Stanley said. "She hated me so."

"Hated you!" my mother cried. "Mary Rose *hated* you? Stanley, what are you talking about?"

"She did!" Uncle Stanley said. "I remember. She hated me."

"Stanley, you know how kids fight, and the three of us were no different from other kids. You were too little when she died to remember, but she didn't hate you. Sure, sometimes she whined and fussed—I do remember, but she was so—so weak and defenseless. She really was a very delicate, dreamy child."

"She hated me," Uncle Stanley said. "And when you or Mama weren't around, she'd tease me and pinch me and tell me horrible stories about how I was going to die."

"Stanley, you can't remember . . ."

"She used to say that Mama loved me the best, and you loved me the best, and Papa loved me the best, and nobody loved her. She said it all the time, Veronica. You're the one who doesn't remember."

My mother didn't say anything.

"Papa used to smoke those cigars sometimes, and if I was around, he'd give me the ring to put on my finger. It didn't mean anything special. I guess he figured I was the only one young enough to want to play with them. I didn't even particularly want them, but then she'd come after me, and try to get them away from me. She'd wheedle and threaten me, or hit me, or scare me, and sooner or later, I'd give them to her."

"I didn't know," my mother said, "but kids fight, and older ones are jealous of younger ones. Look at Olivia. You can see she's jealous of Margaret. But they grow out of it."

"If they live," said Uncle Stanley. "But when they die, they die with it."

"So it's over with . . ." my mother started to say.

"No, it's not over with," Uncle Stanley said. "I'm not over with it. I'm thirty-six years old, I have a wife and five children, and I'm still afraid of Mary Rose."

"The important thing," said my mother, "is that you told me, and I think you'll probably feel better now. It's always good to get things off your chest. You see them in perspective. Maybe even through somebody else's eyes. To me, Mary Rose was a pathetic, vulnerable child who was more to be pitied than feared. Poor, little thing! I guess if she had lived, it would have all worked out for her. She would have grown up—like the rest of us—maybe even better. Who knows? Look how she saved your life and how she alerted everybody in the building. Stanley, you have to admit she had some wonderful things in her."

Here is where I began crying. Softly, so nobody could hear me. Crying for myself and Mary Rose.

"She didn't," Uncle Stanley said.

"Didn't what?"

"Didn't save my life, and didn't save anybody else's either."

"Stanley! Stanley!" my mother said, and her voice sounded scolding. "You know she did."

"She didn't," Uncle Stanley cried.

I was crying louder now in the closet, but nobody heard me.

"Do you remember," Uncle Stanley continued, "how you used to stay with me at night when Mama and Papa were away?"

"Sure I remember," my mother said. "I could never get you to go to bed. You'd think of a million excuses to get out of bed, and I'd have to tell you lots of stories before you'd settle down."

"I used to like it when they were away because it was so much fun when you took care of me, but once in awhile, you weren't home either, and then Mary Rose had to look after me."

"There was a party that night," my mother said, "at Lorraine Jacob's house. It was the first time I danced with a boy. I remember."

"And Papa smoked a cigar. He gave me the ring, and when they left she wanted it. He never knew she wanted those rings so much. If he knew he would have given them to her. Isn't it funny how he never knew? How I never told him, and how she never told him? But she always knew when I got one.

"That night, all night, she tried to get it from me. First she said I could play with her lipstick samples. I said no. Then she said she'd be my slave for half an hour. I said no. Then she said a vampire would come and suck the blood from my neck that night, and that she knew the magic word to make sure he'd come. I said no. She pulled my hair, and smacked my face, and kicked my knee. So I ran into the bedroom, got into bed and cried, but I wouldn't let her have it.

"I guess I fell asleep, because the next thing I remember, she was standing over me, and I knew as soon as I opened my eyes that she'd pulled the ring off my finger. The first thing I said was, 'Mary Rose, give me back my ring!'

"'I haven't got it, stupid,' she cried.

"She was holding the box under her arm, but she

spread out her fingers to show me the ring wasn't on any of them.

" 'You put it somewheres,' I yelled. 'Give me back my ring or I'll tell Mama.'

" 'Shut up!' she said. 'I put it in my box to keep it safe. There's a fire, so get up! Here!' she handed me the box. 'Go on, take it downstairs. I'm going to get my other boxes, and then I'll come too. Hurry!'

"I started crying, so she pulled me out of bed, and gave me a push. I could smell the fire, and see smoke coming out of the kitchen.

" 'Take the box, stupid,' she said. 'And you better not drop it or lose it or I'll get you good.'

"Then she went into your bedroom, and I never saw her again, except at the window. All she could think about was getting her boxes out safely. That's all that mattered to her. Not me and not anybody else. She went back to get her boxes, and that's why she was trapped."

"But didn't she come out into the hall with you?" asked my mother. "Didn't she ring all those bells, and tell the people to get out?"

"No," Uncle Stanley said, "she didn't."

"But people said she did. They said she rang the bells and warned them. It wasn't only one person who said so."

"She didn't," Uncle Stanley said. "I know she didn't. She never came out of that room."

"But people heard her."

"No," Uncle Stanley said. "They didn't hear her. They heard me."

"Stanley!"

"I rang all the bells going down, and I shouted 'Help!' and 'Fire!' Mama always used to smack me when I rang bells, but this was one time I knew she wouldn't smack me. So I rang the bells, and I was happy, and I held on to her box, but later, when I got outside, and there was all that yelling and screaming, and the smoke was in my eyes, later I wasn't happy. And then somebody looked up at the window, and she was standing there, and somebody else said she had rung the bells, and warned everybody. It all got mixed up in my mind. I thought she'd be mad at me because I rang the bells, and I held on to that box because I didn't want her to be mad over that too. I didn't know what it meant when the building collapsed. I was only afraid she'd come after me, and people tried to take away the box, and I couldn't tell them."

"But, Mama . . . ," my mother said.

"So after awhile it was too late to say anything. And Mama began to make a whole fantasy out of Mary Rose, and what happened. So I never told her, and I never will. I don't want to either, because even now, it's hard for me to talk about Mary Rose. But I could never name a child of mine after her, because to be perfectly honest with you, Veronica, I never really liked Mary Rose."

I must have been crying very loud by then. Maybe I was even screaming. Because suddenly the light in the closet was on, and Uncle Stanley was saying, "But, Mary Rose! What are you doing here?"

My mother was saying, "I knew this would happen. I told you over and over again, one of these days you were going to hear something you weren't going to want to hear. It serves you right."

But I was crying so hard that after awhile she picked me up, and sat down on that bench with the lavender and white striped cushions, and rocked me back and forth in her lap like I was a little kid, and didn't say anything at all.

10

My father came out to get me the next morning. I couldn't stop crying so he took me back to my grandmother's place. He brought me upstairs to my bedroom, and said I should change into my pajamas, and get into bed. He was going downstairs to make some rice pudding. He said he would tell my grandmother that I had the flu, and that he was going to stay home the whole day to take care of me.

I got into bed, and put my hot, swollen face down on the cool, dry pillow, and felt it go wet underneath me.

"Mary Rose! Mary Rose!"

My grandmother was whispering to me from the doorway. This was the first time since the accident that she'd come up the stairs.

"Grandma," I sobbed, "you're not supposed to be climbing up the stairs all by yourself." I tried to wipe my eyes so she wouldn't know I was crying but my whole face was wet.

"Don't worry about that, Mary Rose," she said, walking over to the bed. "What's hurting you, darling? Why are you crying like that?"

"Oh, everything," I said truthfully, wiping one eye and feeling tears oozing out of the other.

"Is the pain in your stomach? Is it on your right side?"

"No, Grandma. Please don't worry. I'll be fine."

There were worry lines all over her face as she stood over me. She put a hand on my forehead, and I thought to myself how she would be crying too if she knew what I knew. It made me angry at her. I wanted her to go away.

"I just want to go to sleep." I lay down and turned away from her.

"Yes, that's the best thing. And, Mary Rose . . ."

"What?"

"How would you like me to ask your father to bring up the TV set so later when you wake up, you can watch TV? I could come up and watch too."

"No! I don't want to watch TV! I hate TV!" I just wanted her to go away, and leave me alone.

"Oh!" That's all she said. I could hear her moving away from the bed. I knew she was feeling bad, and I also knew that I was the one who made her feel bad. It made me feel even worse.

I sat up in bed, and the tears were really streaming down my face. "Grandma!" I cried. She hurried back, sat down on the bed, and put her arms around me.

"My sweet girl!" she said, kissing me a few times on different parts of my face. Then she patted my back, and I patted hers, and we both felt better. After awhile I lay down again and my grandmother stood up and said, "You take a good rest now, and you'll feel better. You're not hot, but I still think your father should call the doctor. He says he has to make rice pudding. I don't know why he can't call the doctor *and* make the rice pudding. Or even why he has to make rice pudding at all. Jello is much lighter on the stomach. But there are some people who you just can't talk to . . ."

By the time my grandmother left, I had stopped crying. I was exhausted. My face felt like it was all puffed up, and my body ached like I had Charlie horse. It was good being in bed. Later, when my father came upstairs with a dish of rice pudding, I began to feel better.

Not good. Just better. Better than horrible. It's like being miserable, but not as miserable as you used to be. But still miserable.

I sat up in bed, and my father handed me the dish. "Eat, eat," he said softly. "You'll feel better."

How many years had he been saying the same thing? He watched me eating. It was so good. I hadn't had any breakfast. "Slow down!" he said. "Don't gulp like that. You'll get a stomach ache."

When I finished, he took away the dish and asked if I could sleep now. He thought it would be the best thing if I could take a nap. I'd feel like a new person when I woke up.

"Oh, Daddy," I said. "Did you hear? Did Mom tell you what Uncle Stanley said?"

My father shook his head. "I never liked it," he said. "I told your mother, right away, when you were born. Why name a beautiful, new, little girl after somebody dead and gone? Why name her after anybody for that matter?"

"But that's not the point, Daddy."

"It is the point. The dead is the dead, and the living is the living, and most important of all is that each person should be himself or herself, and nobody else. A dead sister—what's that? I have five living sisters—three of them beautiful, and one of them good and charming as well as beautiful. Did I say name this baby after my sister, Dolores, because she's good and charming and beautiful? No! Because she is she, and you are you, and somebody who died in a fire thirty years ago is somebody else, and somebody who died is gone and finished."

I started to cry again, and my father said, "No, no, never mind me! I'm upset, and I'm upsetting you too. The important thing is that it's over. Forget it, Mary Rose! Forget the whole business!"

"It's not over," I said. "It'll never be over. I thought

136

she was so great, so good and noble and she was mean and horrible, and she never even saved those people. And worst of all . . ." I was really crying, ". . . worst of all, I'm stuck with her name, with Mary Rose. It's a terrible name. I hate it."

My father put the empty dish of rice pudding down on the floor, and sat down on the bed. "But it's not her name anymore. It's your name."

"No, it's her name. And she was mean and selfish and jealous. Why should I have to be named for somebody like that?"

"First of all," my father said, "it's your name, not hers. There must be other people in this world named Mary Rose too. Each of those people is Mary Rose— different and apart from any other Mary Rose."

"But, Daddy . . ."

"Wait, I'm not finished. That's number one. You are Mary Rose and Mary Rose in Pennsylvania is Mary Rose too, but different from you, and Mary Rose in Egypt . . ."

"Oh, Daddy, there's no Mary Rose in Egypt."

"How do you know? She could be the daughter of an American doctor in Cairo, or an actress who lives in Port Said. But, anyway, that's just number one. Number two is—how can you be so sure that Mary Rose was mean and horrible?"

"Because Uncle Stanley said so."

"Maybe Uncle Stanley thought she was, but your grandmother didn't."

"Grandma's just making it all up—about how beautiful and kind and super Mary Rose was. It's a lot of baloney."

"And your mother didn't think she was mean and horrible."

"Maybe not, but she thought Mary Rose was a 'poor, little thing' who was different from everybody else. It's just as bad."

"But it's different," my father said. "It's different from what Stanley said, different from what your grandmother said, different from what you thought. Maybe if you talked to other people who knew her, they would tell you something different too."

"And she didn't save anybody's life. Uncle Stanley did."

"And how can you be sure of that?"

"He said he was the one who rang all the bells going down the stairs, not her."

"*He* said he was the one. But everybody else said she did. I don't say he wasn't telling the truth. I only say how can you be sure his story is the right one? Or the only one. How can you trust to the memories of a frightened six-year-old child? How can you be sure that even if he did ring the bells going down the stairs, she might not have gone up the stairs and rung the bells there? I just say how can you be so sure his story is the only one to believe?"

"I'm so mixed up," I said. "How can you believe anybody? The way you're talking, I'll never find out what happened or what she was like."

"And that's all right too," said my father. "Just think about yourself. Suppose your grandmother was asked to say what you were like. She'd say you were the most beautiful, intelligent and wonderful girl in the world, right?"

"Along with Pam, Jeanette, Margaret and Olivia."

"Right. But she'd say that. If someone asked your mother, she might say you weren't too bad, but you did have this little habit of listening in to other people's conversations. Right? And Manny or Ray would say you were a pest."

"Not all the time."

"And maybe Pam would say you were fun to be with, and Miss Winkler, your old math teacher would say you weren't very bright, but maybe Miss O'Neil, the art teacher, would say you were."

"And what would you say, Daddy?" I was feeling sleepy.

"I?" said my father. "I would say you . . . you . . . were the most wonderful . . . rice pudding eater in the world."

"Oh, Daddy!"

"So be fair. *That* Mary Rose has been dead for

thirty years, and she's not here to speak for herself. If she was, she could tell you what really happened, and what she really was like. But she's dead. So leave her be. Let her rest in peace. That's what it means— you know—rest in peace. It means the dead should rest in peace from the living, and vice versa."

I was really feeling sleepy now, but my father was all wound up, the way he usually gets when something excites him. He started talking about all the dead people who'd been wronged by the living, and all the living people who were persecuted by the dead. As an artist, he said, you had to forget the past and live in the present. Who cared what Cézanne or Rembrandt or Michelangelo thought? Not him! He cared only for what he thought, and, more important, for what he did. Sure, he said, he liked to look at their paintings, but now was now, and you'd never catch him painting Adam and Eve on a ceiling upside down, or spending years painting the same mountain over and over again. Not him! Let the dead bury the dead. The past was the past, and now was now, and when he painted, he said thank you very much to all the great painters of the past and, "Scram now, and let me work!"

I fell asleep.

I slept the whole day. And I dreamed about her. About Mary Rose. But I don't remember what. Only that I woke up at night again. Maybe it was one o'clock, maybe not. But everybody in the house was sleeping. Nearly everybody.

I jumped up and opened the door, and there she was, bending over, listening in.

"Mary Rose," I yelled, "you've been listening in to my dreams."

"Well, you've been listening in to mine," she said. She walked into the room, and looked at everything —at the curtains, at the bed, at the chest, at the mirror.

"You're not real," I said. "You're black and white, like in the newspaper. You're just a dream I'm having."

She was looking all around. "Where is it?" she said.

"Where is what?"

"My box."

"It's at Uncle Stanley's house."

"I want it back," she said. "That's why I came."

"I don't have it," I said. "You'll have to go there to get it."

"OK." She started walking out of the room.

"Mary Rose!" I called, "Mary Rose!"

"Yes?" She turned around, and waited for me to ask my question. I can't really say what she looked like. She was smaller than me, but she was like that picture in the newspaper, so nothing was clear about her, except I knew she was Mary Rose.

"Why do you need that box?"

"It's the only one I don't have." She sounded impatient.

"But why do you need it now?"

"You really are stupid," she said. "*Now* is the time I need it, not any other time."

"But why?"

"Because I've got everything set up right. The countries, the houses, the clothes—everything I need, except for the jewelry and my picture."

"Your picture? You mean the newspaper picture?"

"No! No! My picture of me, my real picture. It's in my jewelry box."

I knew she meant that picture of the sexy, redheaded woman with the big, fake diamond ring on her finger.

"But Mary Rose, you didn't look like that," I told her. "You didn't look anything like that."

"Yes, I did," she said. "I looked exactly like that. And once I get my box back, I will look like that again." She pointed a finger at me, and her voice sounded frightened. "You didn't do anything to it, did you? Is it still there?"

"Yes, it's still there. Everything is still there. I didn't hurt anything. But, Mary Rose . . ."

"What?" She was moving out of the door.

"Mary Rose, please, just tell me, is it true what Uncle Stanley said about you? Is it true what he said about that night?"

"What night?" She was moving quickly through the door.

"The night of the fire."

"What fire?" she said, and then she was gone.

I called, "Mary Rose! Mary Rose!" after her, but she didn't come back.

My mother came back the next day. She didn't tell me what happened to Mary Rose's box, and I didn't ask. She did say that she didn't mean to rub it in, but she hoped I understood now how wrong and dangerous it was to listen in to conversations not intended for my ears. I said yes I did understand. That was good, she said, and she also hoped that meant I wouldn't do it again. But she didn't wait for an answer. She is not the kind of grownup who likes to trap people. I am glad I have her for a mother and not somebody like Aunt Claudia.

My mother said she thought maybe the best thing would be to talk about Mary Rose, and discuss exactly what Uncle Stanley had said. But I said no. I told her not to worry, I wasn't going to say anything to Grandma or to anyone else for that matter, but I told her I didn't want to talk about Mary Rose.

"You will when the hurt wears off a little," said my mother, "and you'll feel better when you do."

But she didn't press me.

She's wrong. I don't think I ever will want to talk about Mary Rose. Even though I am hurting. But it's not for me I'm hurting now. It's for Mary Rose. The way I hurt for Pam or Grandma or somebody I love very much. When they feel bad I feel bad too, and now I'm feeling bad for Mary Rose. Because she was a person. I know that now, and I know that there were lots of times that she felt bad, and whatever she was or is, I can feel that hurting even after thirty years.

My mother is wrong and my father is wrong too. I'm not going to forget her, like he said. I'm not going to sweep her out from inside me like yesterday's dust. But I'm not going to pick on her either, or listen to other people pick on her. They all think because she's dead and can't defend herself, they can say anything they like about her, and I won't let them.

The truth is the only thing I care about. Like I said before, I am a very truthful person, and the truth about Mary Rose is one thing I'll never know. Except that she was a person. But I don't want to hear a lot of different people saying a lot of different things about her. I don't want to have to tell them off. Because it won't be true what they're saying, and she's not here to stick up for herself. And even if she was, she'd be as bad as the rest of them. I know, if she was here, she'd say she looked just like that sexy, red-headed woman in her box. And then I'd have to tell her off too.

11

"We burned it," Pam was saying. "Next day, after your father came and got you, and my father went off to work, we burned it. It was your mother's idea. She didn't really tell me what got you so hysterical, or why my father was so upset. She just said she and I had to look out for the two of you—that's my father and you. But she didn't say it had to be a secret either, so I guess it's all right to tell you."

"I don't want to talk about it," I said. "I told you that before."

"But that's silly," said Pam. "You'll feel better if you talk about it."

"No, I won't. And I don't want to."

"Well, what will you do when Grandma starts in? Because she always does. You can't tell her you don't want to talk about it."

"*She* can talk about it, but I don't have to. And I don't have to listen either. I have a way of not listening when I don't want to. Everybody thinks I am listening, but I'm not."

"I can do that too," said Pam. "But anyway, I'm glad you're not going to talk about Mary Rose anymore. It was boring the way you kept going on and on about her."

I didn't say anything.

"About how great she was!"

I still didn't say anything.

"It was exciting burning her box with your mother. It was like she was one of those evil ghosts, and she wouldn't leave off tormenting people until everything that belonged to her was destroyed. I read a story like that . . ."

"You stop it, Pam!" I yelled.

"Stop what?"

"You stop picking on her! You leave her alone!"

"Are you crazy?" Pam said. "I thought you didn't care about her anymore. I thought you weren't going to talk about her anymore."

"I'm not," I shouted, "but you are."

"You know something, Mary Rose?"

"What?"

"I think you love her just as much as you always did. I don't think you've changed at all."

"Can we stop talking about her?" I yelled. "All I want to do is stop talking about her. And you keep on talking."

"OK, OK," Pam said, "stop shouting! I know you're still upset, so let's just drop it. Of course, if anybody *should* be upset, I guess it really should be me. I know that you looked in the box when you found it, even though you promised . . ."

Sometimes she sounds like her mother, but I love her anyway. So I didn't argue with her. I just said nicely, "Why don't you shut your face, Pam, and I'll show you the chair downstairs with the secret foot-rest."

Most of the company was sitting around the dining room table, drinking coffee and eating my father's coconut cream pie.

"But, Luis," my Aunt Claudia was saying, "wouldn't you agree that space and time have become the chief concerns of the twentieth-century painter?"

I don't know whether my father agreed or not. Pam and I walked into the living room, and she said, "This is a pretty room. The whole house is pretty. It's not very big, but it's pretty."

"Here, look at this." I showed her the two old, matching club chairs on either side of the fireplace. Both of them were covered in a faded blue material.

"They look exactly alike, right?"

"I guess so."

"But see, you sit in this one, and you can press the front of this arm as much as you like, and nothing

149

happens. But go and sit in the other one. Go ahead, Pam."

She sat down, facing me.

"Now, feel around the front of the left arm. Do you feel anything?"

"No . . . yes . . . a little bump."

"Press it!"

She pressed it, and a footrest jumped out from the bottom of the chair.

"Hey, that's neat," Pam said.

She put her feet up on the footrest, leaned back on the chair, and smiled at me.

"It's great that you've got this little house," she said. "I think my mother might even let me come and spend a weekend with you."

"When?"

"Why don't you ask her—today."

"OK, I will."

"No. Wait. Maybe you better ask *your* mother first, and then she can ask my mother."

"OK."

"I hope she'll let me come. She doesn't have anything against your mother, and she really likes your father."

"She does?"

"Yes. She's always telling my father how creative and original he is even though she says she doesn't like most of his paintings."

"That's all right. Most people don't."

"But she keeps telling my father what a great companion he must be, and she just knows he's not the kind of man who watches baseball games on TV all the time, and only talks about sports or his job."

"No, my father never watches baseball games on TV. He likes 'Mannix' and 'Mission Impossible'—programs like that."

The baby began to cry. He was in the little sunroom, off the living room. I ran into the dining room, and said, "Aunt Claudia, can I pick him up. Please, Aunt Claudia, I'll be very careful."

She was getting up from the table.

"Well . . ." she said.

"Sure you can pick him up," my Uncle Stanley said. "But he's pretty heavy for a guy not even a month old yet."

Aunt Claudia was half up and half down.

"I'll be careful," I said.

My mother stood up, and said, "You sit for a while, Claudia. I'll go along with the girls."

"Oh, Mom, I can handle him myself," I said, as we walked into the sunroom.

"I'm sure you can, Mary Rose, but I think Aunt Claudia would be more comfortable if I was along."

"I don't think so," Pam said. "She doesn't think anybody can take care of him the way she can."

The baby was on his stomach, doubling up his legs

under him like he was trying to go somewhere but he didn't know the way, and he couldn't get started even if he did. His little fists were clenched and digging into the car bed mattress. He was wearing a bright blue creeper with white pompons on the feet.

I put my hands under him, and my mother said, "Remember to support his head. That's right."

I brought him up, and held him crooked in my arms. His bright, blue eyes opened wide, and his mouth made little sucking noises.

My grandmother came into the room, and stood next to me, looking down at the baby. "Hello, Ralphie, hello, dolly, hello, you sweet, little, nice, big man . . . you little Stanley, you funny, good-for-nothing, beautiful boy of a baby, you . . ." She went on and on, and my mother laughed and made little kissing noises over him.

Suddenly I felt the baby pull himself very stiff in my arms. His face got crimson, and he started to yell— loud.

Aunt Claudia came in, unbuttoning her blouse. She took the baby away from me, sat down and began nursing him.

The rest of us went back into the dining room. Pam poked my arm with her elbow, and motioned with her head in my mother's direction.

"Mom," I said, "can Pam stay over for the week- end?"

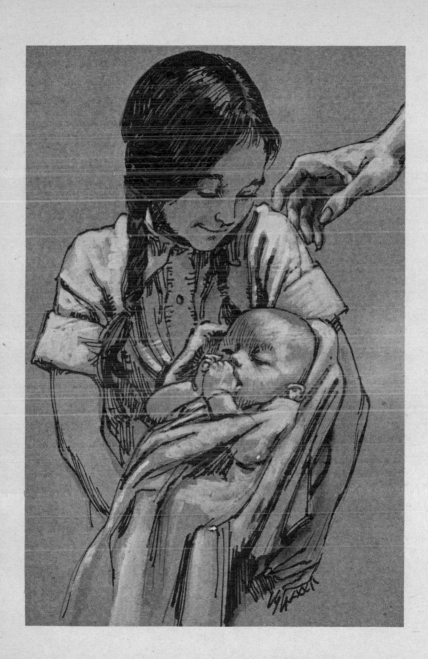

"Yes," my mother said.

Pam pushed my arm again, and I said, "Well, will you ask Aunt Claudia?"

"I did," said my mother. "It's all right."

Pam said slowly, "She said I could? Today? She said I could stay over?"

"Yes," my mother said. "You can stay over until Thursday, as a matter of fact. Your mother wants to do some shopping with you before school opens, so I promised we'd get you home by then."

"I'll have another piece of pie, Luis," said my grandmother.

"Four whole days!" Pam said to me. "I wasn't even sure she'd let me stay overnight."

"Isn't it great!" I said. "We'll have a ball."

"I suppose," my grandmother said, "you use that instant vanilla pudding to make this pie."

"No," said my father, "I start from scratch. Is there any more coffee?" he called into the kitchen. Manny and Ray were doing the dishes. Saturday is their day, although when we have company, everybody is supposed to help.

I walked into the kitchen. "Is there any more coffee, slaves?" I asked.

Ray was washing the dishes, and Manny and Philip were taking the garbage out. Actually, they weren't taking the garbage out, but they nearly were. Philip had the back door open, and Manny was standing in the doorway, holding a large bag of garbage with a big, grease stain all over the top. He looked as if he was on his way out to put the bag in the garbage can. But he wasn't. He was standing there, arguing with Philip, my half brother.

"Don't tell me what I said," Manny was saying, moving his arms up and down.

"I'm not telling you what you said," Philip said. "I'm telling you what I heard. And I heard you say . . ."

"Watch out, Manny, that bag is going to fall."

Philip laughed. He's twenty-two, and very handsome. My mother says my father looked like that when he was young, but it's hard to believe. Philip is an actor. When he can find jobs, he's an actor. The rest of the time, he works in the post office, or in a service station, or he doesn't work at all. Like now. He's in between jobs, and he doesn't have any money. For the past week, he's been staying with us, and I hope he stays with us all the time. I mean, I hope he finds a good acting job, but stays with us anyway. It's fun having Philip around. My father's happy too. He and Philip don't talk a lot, but my father's just happy that he's here. Philip doesn't talk much with anyone, except Manny. And he and Manny argue most of the time. But they're always looking for each other to argue with, so I guess they must enjoy it. When he's not arguing with Manny, Philip plays Monopoly with me. We've been playing every day since he came, and we never even put the board away.

Manny went on out through the door, and you could hear him lifting the garbage can lid, and dropping the bag into the can.

"I'll bring the coffee in," I told Ray.

"OK, and then why don't you come back, and give me a hand. These two jokers are so busy yakking, they're no help at all."

"How can you say that?" Philip asked. "I did all the pots."

"Did what to all the pots?" Ray muttered.

Manny came back into the kitchen. He was talking even before he came through the door. "I may have said that for *me* school was a necessity, but I never made a blanket prescription for the whole world like you said I said."

"See what I mean?" Ray said.

I carried the coffee into the dining room, and poured some coffee for my grandmother and my father. Uncle Stanley and my mother didn't want any more.

Pam was sitting at the table looking unhappy. You could see she was busy thinking her own thoughts, and wasn't listening to what the rest were talking about.

"She doesn't mind my going," Pam said, "because she's got the baby. Since *he* was born she doesn't care what I do or where I go."

"But, Pam," I said, "that's great, and we've got four whole days."

"I know, I know," she said, "but she never would have let me go like that before."

Aunt Claudia came back into the room. She was smiling. My grandmother said, "Is the baby sleeping?"

"Uh, huh."

"He's some baby!" said my grandmother. "He's one of a kind."

She and my Aunt Claudia even smiled at each other. My Aunt Claudia started saying how the baby was eating so much, she didn't even know if it was good for him to eat so much.

Pam got up from the table and walked off into the kitchen.

She's still jealous, I thought. Jealous of the baby. Aunt Claudia kept right on talking about what a great eater the baby was, and then when she finished, Uncle Stanley began talking about what a great sleeper he was. "Not even a month old," said my Uncle Stanley, "and he sleeps through the night." He looked around the table and never noticed that Pam had left.

Even he doesn't notice it. Just like thirty years ago, his father didn't see it either. My grandmother was smiling at Uncle Stanley. Or his mother. Pam is alone in it, I thought. Just like Mary Rose. My Mary Rose. All alone in being jealous and unhappy and desperate. This rotten feeling inside me pushed in all directions, and nearly made my ears pop. I jumped up from the table and ran after her into the kitchen.

Manny and Philip were leaning against the refrigerator, arguing, and Ray was still washing dishes at the sink. Pam was helping him. She was drying the dishes and laughing.

I stood in the doorway, half in the kitchen, and half in the dining room and listened. I could hear the water running in the sink, and the sound of each dish as Pam dried it, and put it on the kitchen table. Ray was speaking very low, and Pam was laughing all the time he was speaking.

"What do *you* know," Philip was saying to Manny, "about anything!"

Nobody noticed me. In the dining room, my grandmother was talking, and the others were drinking coffee or eating pie. There was only her voice and the sounds of spoons in cups or forks on plates.

I was standing right in the middle of it all, listening to them, and nobody noticed me. Everybody was busy talking or laughing or arguing. A few minutes ago Pam was jealous and miserable, and now she was laughing. I had listened to her when she was jealous, and I felt bad. Now I was listening to her laugh, and I felt good. Thirty years ago when Mary Rose was jealous and miserable, weren't there times when she laughed too?

My Aunt Claudia pushed away her plate, and stood up. Everybody else was looking at my grandmother.

"What did I say?" said my grandmother.

I told her. "You said that Uncle Stanley looked tired, and that somebody should see to it that he eats regular meals, gets plenty of rest, and shouldn't have any aggravation when he comes home tired from work."

"*Mary Rose!*" my mother said.

"Did I say that?" my grandmother said, but my father started to laugh, and then Uncle Stanley, and finally Aunt Claudia. She sat down again.

"Mary Rose," my grandmother called, putting out her arm. I came over and sat down next to her, and she pulled my head down on her shoulder and kissed me. "She's got some pair of ears, this girl," said my grandmother.

"Yes, she does," my mother said, looking worried.

But there was nothing to worry about now. This time I had listened to *everything*, so I wasn't feeling bad. And I wasn't hurting for anybody. Not for Pam or for my grandmother or for Mary Rose.

ABOUT THE AUTHOR

MARILYN SACHS, a native of New York City, received a Bachelor of Arts degree from Hunter College and a master's degree in library science from Columbia University. She has worked in the Brooklyn Public Library as a specialist in children's literature, and in the San Francisco Public Library. The author of over twenty-two books for young readers, she is well known for such distinguished titles as *The Bear's House*, a 1971 nominee for the National Book Award, and *Veronica Ganz*, an ALA Notable Book.

Ms. Sachs now lives with her family in San Francisco.